Goodreads Reviews for the Dr Power Books

The Darkening Sky (4.44 Stars)

'Absolutely enjoyed this first novel.'

'I have read many a crime book, but this book was different. I never for one moment guessed how the story would unfold.'

'Loved the way the two main characters (Superintendent Lynch and Dr Power) interacted with one another.'

'Illustrations were brilliantly drawn and brought the characters to life.'

'Thoroughly enjoyed this debut novel from Hugh Greene.'

'Brilliant. Very much enjoyed – a new detective series based in England.'

'It is a good crime and psychological thriller and will keep any reader interested to the end.'

'I love British Mystery stories, and The Darkening Sky is no exception. Well written, with great development of characters; I felt that I knew Power & Lynch personally. I look forward to further volumes in this highly entertaining and somewhat edgy series. Hugh Greene is a writer to start paying attention to in my opinion. Highly recommended.'

The Fire of Love (4.57 Stars)

'Good plot and enjoyable read – away to locate more books in the series.'

'This is a gripping story, I was hooked from the first page and found it difficult to put down. The description of the house and its history and the man who built it was very true to the time and the author really brings it to life.'

'I love the illustration by Paul Imrie on the cover, it is very striking and beautifully drawn as are the black and white illustrations inside.'

'A well written book with a well-thought out storyline, I enjoyed it very much and definitely want to read the next one.'

'There are lots of twists and turns and complex characters to keep the ending hidden from you and difficult to guess.'

'After the first chapter I could not put it down.'

'The illustrations were brilliant evocations of the Power/Lynch world.'

'I love the little links between the books in the illustrations. Dr Power as drawn is quite dishy. I think I'm falling in love with Dr Power!'

'What I enjoy about Hugh Greene novels are not only the illustrations, but the twists.'

'A good read that I would recommend to anyone who enjoys crime novels and psychological thrillers. The writing is constantly good and interesting.'

The Good Shepherd (4.38 Stars)

'I was attracted by the cover of this book, which I thought it very striking and enigmatic.'

'There was drama and suspense and a nice twist at the end. It was quite compulsive, I felt I had to read more to see what happened next.'

'It is a very enjoyable and intriguing read. Well-written, it evokes the spirit of the times, the mid-nineties.'

'I enjoyed this book. The characters were interesting and I felt the book was well researched.'

'The story builds well with excellent attention to detail paid to the places that the main characters visit.'

'The pace of plot was gripping, and makes me want to know what is next. The illustrations were fantastic, and really added to the story.'

'An excellent read, loved it.'

'I was hooked from the first paragraph.'

Also by Hugh Greene

The Darkening Sky

The Fire of Love

Schrödinger's God

Omnibus of Three Novels in a Single Volume
The Dr Power Mysteries

Short Story Collection
Dr Power's Casebook

The Good Shepherd

A Dr Power Murder Mystery

Hugh Greene

Illustrated by Paul Imrie

A catalogue reference for this book is available from the British Library

ISBN 10: 1503104079
ISBN 13: 978-1503104075

First Edition Published Worldwide in February 2015

Typeset in Cambria
Proofreading and typographic design by Julie Eddles

www.hughgreene.com
twitter: @hughgreenauther

I am the good shepherd: the good shepherd giveth his life for the sheep. But he that is a hireling, and not the shepherd, whose own the sheep are not, seeth the wolf coming, and leaveth the sheep, and fleeth; and the wolf catcheth them, and scattereth the sheep.

The hireling fleeth, because he is a hireling, and careth not for the sheep.

The Gospel According to St. John,
The Holy Bible. King James Version.

ONE

The sea and the sky above it were both a uniform grey. A thin beam of sunlight pierced the leaden clouds of dawn highlighting the whiteness of the boat as it rose and sank on the waves. For days, the boat had sat between the empty disc of water and the empty dome of sky. Now, the disc of sea included the windswept rocks of the Welsh coast, and the empty boat nudged its lonely course ever closer to land towards the mouth of the River Dee. Ahead of it lay the opening in a harbour wall. Below stairs, in a tiny galley, cups and plates shifted as the boat rolled to and fro. A brown smudge of dried blood on the stairway bore silent and unheeded testimony to recent events on the deserted vessel. The bedding of the single berth in the bow was cold now and had been for days. No-one had slept there through the lonely days and nights since the struggle. Under the sleeping bag and under the mattress itself was a slim laptop computer, hidden in a hurry whilst in mid-task, now silent, its battery long-dead.

Drifting with the tide, the boat was coming back to safe harbour, as if by homing instinct, to tell its tale to those who would listen.

* * *

There were packing cases piled full of books, still scattered around Power's office. The cases had lain unopened for two months. Somehow Power couldn't bear to unpack and fill the drab shelves that lined his new office in the general hospital. He had liked the old hospital. The old building had felt solid, with decades of solidity in its very bricks and bones. It had only just had millions lavished on a refurbishment, and now it lay empty, devoid of patients and staff, and curiously the newly renovated county asylum was being sold to developers at a knockdown price. Power scented that a profit was being made by someone and he viewed his new quarters with little more than contempt.

Power had unpacked his computer, of course. He was practically addicted to his email and the world-wide-web. His colleagues shook their heads when he said the relatively newly arrived internet would transform their lives. He logged in to Windows 95 and wound up the fizzing modem and invoked the spells within to join the Internet to see if any emails had arrived since his morning fix at home. The hospital had grudgingly put in a phone line for his 16k modem. Only one new email. A doctor who'd studied with him at University, who had rung round and compiled a list of email addresses for the last ten years' worth of graduates from Power's medical school. Not every doctor had an email address. But there was a list of about two hundred names. Maybe ten percent of the graduates had email. Power thought about deleting the email. Why would he want to email these people? The computer cursor hovered above the on screen delete button. He paused. A thought that you never knew when this sort of information might come in useful stayed his hand. He revoked the email's death sentence and instead saved it securely.

He turned his attention to the post in his in-tray.

His secretary, Laura, poked her head around the door and surveyed the consultant as he sat at his desk amidst the boxes. "You must unpack, Carl. It looks untidy for one thing and as if you're just about to leave us for another."

Power nodded. "I don't like the canteen here either; soggy chips."

Laura was a slim, pretty, young woman with cropped blonde hair and jade green eyes, which always seemed to twinkle when Power was about although he never seemed to notice. "I like soggy chips, Carl." Laura smiled. "Soggy chips and gravy! There's nothing better, is there? And there's more going on here than at the old hospital. There are more specialities here – Medicine, Surgery. Doesn't it make you feel like a proper doctor now?"

"I am a consultant psychiatrist," said Power. "They never let you feel like a proper doctor. Although I guess, it must be worse for psychologists. I heard one surgeon at lunch yesterday say that psychologists should be gassed like badgers. Seemed a trifle extreme to me." He paused. "And the canteen is so focussed on meat , Laura – sausage rolls, pasties, roast beef, lamb stew, gammon and chips, ham omelettes, beef, pork, beef, pork, pork, pork . . . You'd think they'd never heard of BSE. Even McDonalds banned serving British beef."

"Are you still thinking of becoming some vegan hippy, Carl. Just to avoid BSE?" She tutted. "Cheer up. There's a new Government in now. Things are looking up."

"Mr Blair is just more of the same old same old . . . and he just makes me cringe. And they are no different. Blair would privatise your granny. They were even floating the idea of charging for NHS services in *The Times* this morning."

Laura sighed. She tried to keep Power's spirits up, but it was clear that the local mental health service reorganisation with its move to a different Hospital Trust had not helped Power's humour. "Cheer up, Dr Power. I have news of privates." Laura used the term privates for signalling private patients.

"I don't like private patients – you know this, they're too much trouble. They pay for an hour of your time and think they own you for life." Power's forays into the world of private medicine hadn't always pleased him in the past, despite the fees. "Phoning you up at all hours," he went on in a disgruntled fashion.

"This is quite different, Carl," said Laura. "This is a commission for a psychiatric report."

"Ah, now that is quite different," said Power. "I quite like those."

"A psychiatric report on a dead person."

Power frowned in a puzzled way. "And how can I interview a dead person for a report? With the services of a medium? What are you getting me into, Laura?"

"Be sensible for five minutes, Dr Power. It's the Coroner

who is commissioning it. He wants you to read through the deceased's GP records and comment on the medication he was taking." Dr Power's frown didn't lift and so Laura said in a wheedling way, "The coroner is offering £250. I said I thought you would agree."

Power nodded, thoughtfully. "Will you help me with it?"

"For my usual percentage, Dr Power, of course."

* * *

Power sat alone at home in Alderley House with the paperwork from the Coroner scattered around him on the sofa. A chorus by Respighi was playing on the radio in a distant room. Evening sunlight poured through the window, but Power felt cold and sobered by what he had read. The notes from the Coroner included the Home Office pathologist's post mortem report and the deceased's medical records from the General Practitioner. The medical notes sketched out the deceased's life from cradle to grave, and somehow made the deceased real to Power. Power's promise to provide a report for the Coroner no longer seemed an abstract task. It felt now as if the deceased was there in the room with Power, looking over the doctor's shoulder.

Up to a fortnight before, Dr Fergus McAdams had been a busy and highly respected research scientist for a local outpost of an international pharmaceutical company. A Ph.D. from the University of Oxford. He had amassed a distinguished and prodigiously long list of publications on infectious disease and parasites, biochemistry, pharmacology and pharmacokinetics. Now his mortal existence was apparently limited to a cold and waterlogged corpse in a mortuary chest cabinet. Power shuddered as he read the details of the Pathologist's report. Such details rarely entered a psychiatrist's work. Power prided himself on keeping his patients alive.

Dr McAdams's remains had been retrieved by the police from a beach at Anglesey following a panicked and stammering phone call from a holidaymaker who had been walking his terrier on the sands. The pathologist concluded that Dr McAdams had not drowned but that he had been dead or very near dead when he entered the water. Subsequent testing of his blood suggested exceedingly high levels of alcohol and antidepressants. Stomach contents included several dozen tablets and the residue of at least a litre of red wine. The thought made Power feel a little sickly. He pushed his remaining chicken and avocado sandwich away, and he set his glass of wine aside.

The GP notes chronicled a life from birth by forceps at St. Mary's Hospital (7 pounds and 6 ounces) to an attendance four weeks before death. At his final encounter with the GP, McAdams had been complaining of some work stress and seeking a sleeping tablet, which the GP had refused. Power followed the young McAdams through letters from a school doctor about bat-ears, surgery at the children's hospital, a broken leg from a fall from an apple tree, food poisoning as a student, a single venereal infection after a one-night stand, various vaccinations for smallpox as a child, and similar immunisations for occupational health for hepatitis, tetanus and typhoid; all this and an occasional duel with diarrhoea and vomiting and a skirmish with chest infections suggested a man in relatively good health all his life.

And no hint of mental disorder through the years except for recent work stress and poor sleep.

Hardly the medical history of an incipient suicide.

Power sat back, took a glug of wine and began locking the house up for the night. Outside the wind was blowing through the trees on the Edge, and it was perilously dark. All the locals of the village knew better than to wander so late at night in the woods near the sandstone Edge. Power slid the heavy front door bolt home and somehow his breath caught in his chest. He thought of the darkness, the hidden cliff edges and the uneven shelves of rock that concealed ancient mine workings and shuddered. He tried to resist any thinking about falling and hurried upstairs to his warm bed.

* * *

Where a portion of the cliff face had given way and sheered off into the sea, there was a root dangling out of the earth. Power grabbed it and inched himself further down the cliff. Without warning, the earth abruptly fell away from under his feet. He tried waving his feet about to make a purchase, but there was no purchase to be made in free air. He allowed himself to fall back a few more feet. His right foot found purchase on a small ledge, and he tested it with his weight.

The rock held. He scrabbled and scrabbled at the grass around him to try and get a grip, he turned to look over the edge behind him. To his right there was nothing but a sheer drop to the jagged toothed rocks below. Sea swirled like saliva over the rocks. And then, in this version of the dream, Tuke's sly face loomed over him, safe from a ledge gouged out of the cliff face by the wind and rain. And Tuke was on him, battering at his head as Power tried to gain the safety of solid earth as opposed to the cold briny fingers of the sea, and then the earth beneath his fragile grip slipped downwards. His hands clawed at the cliff. His nails were scrabbling in the dirt for some hold and lost. In this version of the dream, Power fell and fell . . . and inevitably woke gasping for breath. He lay there disorientated, arms flailing about amidst a clumsy, tangled nest of sweat-sodden bedding.

The dreams came when they wished, visiting him as nightly ghosts. He knew there would be no sleep now. Tiredly he rose from his rumpled sheets. His cold tee-shirt stuck to his back as he wandered to the bathroom and started running a shower.

His thoughts ran through the real events of the day with Tuke as he stepped into the warm water and bathed his fevered body.

The warm water that bathed Power now was so different to the cold, dark waves that had reached out for and enveloped the murderer Tuke and had extinguished him. Power had watched him fall with a mixture of horror and a guilty satisfaction that he, not Tuke, had survived. He had seen the body, once or twice, broken and thrown by the angry waves against the sheer rock wall below, and then it had disappeared into the inky fathoms of the deep.

It had taken Power an hour to recover his wits and conquer his fears enough to face the climb back from the ledge to safety and civilisation. He shivered still, his body remembering the cold and the protracted fear for his life.

Warmed by the shower now, he stepped into slippers and rubbed himself with the fluffiest, whitest, comfiest towel money could buy and hurried downstairs for warmth, light and reminders of life; anything to banish the ghosts of his memory from his mind.

Passing through the living room, he saw the Coroner's paperwork and cursed it. The thought of McAdams in the deep dark belly of the sea had opened the way for the ghost of Tuke to grip his dreams and battle Power again. Every time he thought the dream ghosts had gone, they returned with only the slightest invitation – any encounter with a television programme about a trawler or climbing K2 would beckon and summon Tuke from his watery grave in the night following.

And a psychiatrist or not, Power seemingly had no control over his own dreams.

TWO

Dr Carl Power sped down his front drive in Alderley Edge, paused briefly at the road's edge and turned left onto the Macclesfield Road. It was early; the sun was shining and the traffic was light. He made Macclesfield in good time and wandered about the streets of the market town. He always felt slightly nervous ahead of appearing in Court and had travelled into the old silk town much too early.

Power ordered a macchiato coffee at a café across the square from the Town Hall, where the Coroner's Court was. He sat drinking this and munching at a rather mushy pain au raisin and tried his best to concentrate on a copy of *The Guardian*. He kept looking at his watch, however, counting down the minutes, and in the end could not help but read through his psychiatric report for the Inquest, as if he was revising again for a viva examination.

Eventually, he crossed the square and walked inside the dark Victorian atrium and after reading a sign made with press-on letters, climbed the grand staircase. The massive oil portraits of long-dead council politicians watched his progress disdainfully. The Coroner's Court was to be held in a lofty square room laid out with serried ranks of long tables and uncomfortable chairs facing the Coroner's raised desk and seat. Power was the first there and seated himself at the very back.

A few silent and glum family members were ushered in and took their place at the front. Within seconds of their sitting down, a sharp man in a crisp white shirt and black suit, joined them. He began explaining matters to them in a soft, oily voice. He paused in his exposition to make a very pointed and hostile glare at Power. 'Unfriendly,' thought Power to himself and poured a glass of water from a jug on the table nearby. He sipped the water as a distraction.

At the appointed hour, the Court usher asked the assembled people in the Court to rise and the Coroner, Dr Faulkes, entered. He was a small, blue-eyed man with an air of restless authority. He begged the Court to be seated and murmured a few words of comfort to the bereaved relatives and introduced his role and the function of the Court. He went through the facts of the deceased's disappearance, the discovery of his boat and the eventual recovery of the body on the coast of the Wirral peninsula and its eventual identification as Dr McAdams. He explained that as the deceased came from the Cheshire area he was holding the Inquest, rather than the Mersey coroner. Dr Faulkes explained that he would begin with the hearing of professional and expert testimony before other factual witnesses.

Following the Coroner's introduction the toxicologist, Dr Manders, was called. She was a prim, elderly consultant in a twinset and pearls. She carried a large, leather handbag and from its capacious interior withdrew her slim report. The Clerk of the Court gave her a Bible to hold and held a card in front of her for her to read the appropriate oath and swore her in.

"I swear by Almighty God that the evidence I shall give shall be the truth the whole truth and nothing but the truth," said Dr Manders.

The Coroner looked upon her and gave the briefest and most watery of smiles. "Good morning Dr Manders, can you tell us your full name and occupation please?"

"I am Dr Lesley Manders, and I am qualified both as a Home Office pathologist and a toxicologist."

The Coroner, Dr Faulkes, nodded approvingly. "But you did not perform the post-mortem examination; just the toxicology report I believe?"

"That is correct, Sir."

"Can you tell the Court your findings please?"

"Dr McAdams had various prescription drugs, and their metabolites, in his blood and stomach contents, along with a quantity of alcohol."

"What were the relevant drugs, please?" asked the Coroner.

"There were diazepam and amitriptyline tablets in his stomach and small intestine – and these drugs were also reflected in his bloodstream along with their various metabolites."

"And for the benefit of the Court, what are these drugs used for?" asked the Coroner.

"Diazepam is a member of the benzodiazepine group of drugs," explained Dr Manders. "It's a tranquilliser that helped with anxiety and sleep. Amitriptyline is a tricyclic antidepressant – very dangerous in overdose."

"And the levels of these chemicals in Dr McAdams's bloodstream, were they high?"

"Yes."

"How high, please?"

"Enough to cause unconsciousness, to cause respiratory depression and cardiotoxic side effects. The amitriptyline was in excess of 300 ng/mL, levels that would lead to ventricular tachycardia and asystole in most people."

"A potentially fatal dose?"

"Undoubtedly," said Dr Manders.

"I see, would you like to add anything to your evidence?"

"No, Sir."

"Then please can you remain there, Dr Manders, while I ask the family if they have any questions?" asked the Coroner. "I understand that the deceased's sister and family are represented by a solicitor provided by the deceased's employers. An unusual beneficence, Mr er . . ."

The black-suited raven of a solicitor who had glared at Power earlier rose slowly and, with exaggerated gravity, to his feet.

"Thank you, Sir. I am Mr Cousins, I represent the deceased's family. This is Dr McAdams's sister, Mrs Sarah Ferguson. Her husband accompanies her. And I am as you say, retained by Dr McAdams's employers, Howarth-Weaver. We are a family company, although we are a large concern. As a family company, we always look after the family of our employees. It is not unusual for us to take this kind of care."
Dr Faulkes, the coroner, looked rather sceptical, and his eyes

drifted to the rear of the courtroom where a few members of the media sat taking notes.

"Does the family have any questions for Dr Manders, Mr Cousins?"

"No, Sir."

"Then, Dr Manders, I thank you for your evidence; you may stand down, and although you may stay and observe if you so wish, you are also free to go and carry on with your normal business." Dr Manders lost no time in gathering her things into her voluminous bag and vacating the room. Power felt his mouth dry, and he took a gulp of water apprehensively as the Coroner fixed his eyes upon him. "Dr Power? I would like to call you to give evidence, please."

Power reluctantly got to his feet and walked the short distance to the witness box. The clerk brought the copy of the Bible and asked Power to read the oath, "I swear by Almighty God that the evidence I shall give shall be the truth the whole truth and nothing but the truth," he said. Power felt his tongue almost sticking to the roof of his mouth, and he looked about for water. As he was bidden to sit down he poured another glass of water from a nearby pitcher and glugged some down, nervously. Power felt the gaze of the beady eyes of Mr Cousins and the steely blue eyes of the Coroner upon him.

"Dr Power," said the Coroner. "Can you tell us your full name and profession, please?"

"I am Dr Carl Power, a consultant psychiatrist."

"And I thank you for your expert report in Dr McAdams's medical history. If you recall in my instructions, I asked you to consider Dr McAdams's GP records from a psychiatric point of view. And I think that you went a bit further than this?"

"Yes, I was unable to find any reference to a history of depression, or indeed a record of any mental health problems in Dr McAdams's GP notes, and so I spoke to his sister by telephone."

"I see," said the Coroner. "You mention that the notes contain no history of depression, but what about more recent times. Dr McAdams had high levels of an antidepressant in his bloodstream."

"The GP records do not include any prescription for amitriptyline or diazepam."

"I see," said Dr Faulkes. "And please tell the Court – what did you learn from Dr McAdams's sister, Sarah?"

Power finished off a further gulp of water. He was warming to his theme. "I learned that there was no family history of depression or suicide. I learned that Dr McAdams had seemed in good spirits when he was last seen by his sister, Mrs Ferguson."

"I see, Dr Power. I have a witness statement by Sarah Ferguson to the effect that she last saw Dr McAdams some months ago. A person's mental state can change markedly over a few months can't it?"

"Well, yes . . . but Mrs Ferguson also said that Dr McAdams was teetotal. The presence of alcohol in the bloodstream would seem highly unusual, Sir."

"I see, Dr Power," said the Coroner. "I take it, therefore, that you haven't found anything in particular to point towards Dr McAdams being of unsound mind".

" No, nothing."

"And yet the toxicological evidence does point towards an overdose?"

"Well yes," Power had to concede the point.

"Well, Dr Power, I thank you for your evidence – I have no further questions for you. I don't suppose . . ."

Mr Cousins, smart and eager, had leapt to his feet. "The family have some questions, please?" Mr and Mrs Ferguson looked somewhat surprised that Cousins had stood up. What questions Mr Cousins had prepared were probably an equal surprise. Cousins fixed Power with a stare. Power, slightly annoyed by the Solicitor's apparent rudeness, stared defiantly back. As he did so, he wondered whether he could see a discolouration of the Lawyer's left cheekbone. The more Power observed Cousins's face, the more he thought that there was a fading bruise, on the left-hand side, which had in the main been skilfully masked by concealer. Power struggled to remember what he had been taught about giving evidence. Power chose to look at the Coroner instead of the Lawyer. Dr Faulkes gave him a nod of encouragement.

"Dr Power," Cousins began. Power struggled to keep his eyes on the Coroner. "How long have you been a consultant?"

"Five years?" Power sounded vague.

"Five years precisely?"

"Well . . . er . . . no, I . . ."

"Maybe I can assist you? Isn't it four years and ten months, Dr Power?"

"I'm not sure, if you say so?"

"Oh, Dr Power, you're the one who is meant to be the expert. It is your career, not mine; I think? Is it a busy life being a consultant?"

"Well, yes," said Power, wondering where all this was going.

"A bit of a struggle for you, I suppose, and have you had any complaints recently, from ex-patients maybe?"

The Coroner chose to intervene. "Is this pertinent, Mr Cousins? There is no jury here to play to. There is simply no need to take this apparent line of questioning *ad hominem*. I am satisfied that Dr Power is who he says he is and that he has appropriate expertise as a consultant psychiatrist, albeit a relatively young professional. I chose him to provide me with a report. Are you challenging my choice?"

Cousins backtracked sensing that the Coroner would not entertain any attempt to discredit Power. He began again, "Dr Power, I am sure you appreciate how distressed the family are and how further distress might be caused by any inadvertent implications you make about the circumstances of Dr McAdams's death. You seek to imply that Dr McAdams had no record of mental ill health in his GP notes. Does every person with depression contact their GP?"

"Well, no."

"Wouldn't it actually be the case that most people with depression do NOT contact their GP?"

"Well, you see, in looking at the . . ."

"Just answer yes or no, Dr Power. That is all that is required. Is it the case that most people with depression do NOT contact their GP?"

"No, they don't."

"So if most people with depression do not contact their GP, then there would be no record in their notes, would there?"

"No."

"And if an intelligent, scientific person wished to be . . . discreet . . . and treat themselves, is it not possible to acquire the necessary drugs such as antidepressants without seeing their GP? Getting the drugs from a friend or a relative? Or even a pharmacy over this new thing . . . the Internet?"

"Yes, but . . ."

Cousins interrupted and spat out another question. "As for alcohol, Dr Power – isn't secrecy about alcohol a recognised feature of alcohol misuse?"

Power was determined to make a point. "But Dr McAdams was not alcohol dependent."

"You seem very sure. Did you ever meet Dr McAdams?

"No."

"Then just how can you be so sure? Or is this a guess on your part – like when you guessed earlier, on oath, at how long you had been a consultant?"

"I'm just saying that there is no evidence of depression, no evidence of alcoholism, no evidence of suicidal behaviour ever before."

"And yet," the Coroner intervened. "We have evidence from Dr Manders that Dr McAdams had taken alcohol and a large quantity of antidepressants – a dose that he, as a man of science, must have known was potentially lethal?" Cousins beamed. The Coroner was making his points for him.

"Dr Faulkes, sir," the Solicitor went on. "I would like to call a witness in due course". The Coroner frowned. "A senior manager who will testify to conversing with Dr McAdams and to his low mood at work; perhaps Dr Power might like to listen and reconsider his opinion?" The Coroner blinked at the Solicitor, and Dr Power, and the bewildered family.

"An additional factual witness at this stage. Unusual, Mr Cousins?"

"The witness was abroad but has come forward, Sir. I believe that the Court will find his evidence highly relevant."

"Very well," said the Coroner. He turned to Carl Power. "Dr Power I sought your advice as an expert witness on the objective evidence of the GP notes. And you have done this, thank you. I do not require you to listen to this additional evidence, which is for me to consider. I do not wish you to make judgements or speculate on further evidence. Mr Cousins appears to be asking you to concede that Dr McAdams may have taken his life? Can I ask – is that at least possible in your opinion?"

"It is possible," said Power, "but I think it very unlikely for the following reasons. He had no history of severe depression (and the usual natural onset of this condition would have been in his early adult life and have left some traces in his medical record), he had no family history of depression or suicide in relatives and there is no convincing history of any alcohol abuse."

"But there is . . . a possibility?"

"I'd have to say yes."

Cousins looked smugly at Power. The Coroner went on, 'You see, Dr Power, I appreciate your experience, your intuition as it were, but I must confine myself to the facts, which include a physical overdose, and I will be interested to hear this additional evidence from a colleague, as well of course, as evidence from the family. So I thank you for your attendance and evidence. You are released. Please feel free to stay and listen – otherwise you are equally free to go."

With this Power was dismissed. He returned to the table he had sat at before and gathered his things. He was about to leave, to run off – when his curiosity got the better of him and he sat down. Cousins sneered over his shoulder at him, and Power felt unaccountably small. He mused over his performance in the witness box rather as a lion might nurse a wounded paw. He realised how deliberate and how effective the verbal put downs of Mr Cousins had been. On the other hand, he knew that early on in Power's ordeal the Coroner had seen through Cousins's tricks. And there was no jury, it was the Coroner's opinion that mattered.

At the behest of Mr Cousins the factual witness was called and announced as a senior manager of Howarth-Weaver, the pharmaceutical conglomerate. A tall man of about sixty-two took the stand and was sworn in. His suit was as grey as his hair and his eyes were of an equally dull battleship grey. He gave his evidence as Cousins had foretold. He said he managed a group of scientists, although he himself was a business graduate. Dr McAdams had been working in a small team on microbial biology, particularly Plasmodium species. In recent months, there had been problems at work and he had become morose, withdrawn, and his work output had become erratic. He had missed important targets. He sometimes smelt of whisky, and he had once been sent home after lunch for being discernibly drunk.

Dr Faulkes, the coroner, interrupted. "We had heard – before you arrived – that Howarth-Weaver is a very caring company. As a caring manager did you arrange occupational healthcare for Dr McAdams?" Both the Manager and Mr Cousins frowned. This was an unforeseen question. The Manager looked discomfited as the Coroner's question departed from the script. "Well?"

"I'm sorry, but I did not think of it; it was a disciplinary matter."

"And yet you have described clear signs of depression? An illness not a misdemeanour."

The Manager's dead eyes fixed on the Coroner. "I . . . er . . . asked Dr McAdams to see his own GP."

Power did not believe this. It was difficult to see whether the Coroner did.

"And I believe you referred to the team earlier. The team that Dr McAdams was part of. Are they available to give evidence? To corroborate what you are saying?"

"I am sorry Sir; I don't know. The team is no more."

"No more?" The Coroner frowned.

"The team that he was working with have left the company. Their work did not come to any conclusions. Projects begin and end. Some succeed, some don't. This one didn't."

"I would like the names and addresses of these co-workers if you please. Can you furnish my office with them, please?"

"We will try, but I believe that the other members of the team have gone to work abroad."

The Coroner looked at Mr Cousins. "I trust that these names and addresses will be forthcoming?"

Mr Cousins stood up. "We will have those names for you, Sir."

"By the end of tomorrow, if you please. Without fail." Dr Faulkes glared at Cousins, and Power felt somehow reassured. "Well, I think that we have probably heard enough for this morning. This afternoon I will take the family through their evidence if I may. Then we will adjourn the Inquest. I may take further factual evidence or maybe not," he looked at Cousins. And with this the Coroner and the Court rose. The Coroner sought the refuge of his rooms and a good lunch.

Power watched as Cousins herded the family away from him and thought that he would like to speak with McAdams's sister whenever he could.

The next day Cousins phoned the Coroner's office to apologise and say that, with regret and after much effort to try and track them down, the names and addresses of McAdams's team unfortunately could not be provided.

The Coroner recorded an Open Verdict later that week.

* * *

Superintendent Andrew Lynch met Dr Power downstairs in the reception where they had arranged to meet at the Chester city centre Police Headquarters in Nuns Road. He was busy buttoning up his coat and practically pushed his old friend out of the doors in his haste to get outside. "Let's get out of here. We can walk around the walls as we talk." Power assented, but he really had no choice. He followed the elegant figure of the tall police officer as he crossed the road, and they began walking the Roman walls, past the stumpy remains of Chester Castle and the nearby Law Courts.

On the right-hand side the river flowed down below the walls. Power had a fantasy of stopping off at a pub, but Lynch would never drink on duty.

"Perhaps we can stop somewhere for coffee?" Power suggested.

"Maybe," said Lynch, as he strode ahead. "I don't want to be late for Evensong at the Cathedral though. Lynch was a man of habit, and it was already four o'clock. Choral evensong was at five thirty. "It's good to see you though. The wife was asking after you the other day. Are you sleeping any better?"

"I reserve that question for my patients, usually," said Power, thinking back to the nightmare he kept having.

"Physician heal thyself, Luke 4:23," said Lynch, as they came to Bridgegate on the South Wall.

Power grunted and decided to avoid the subject. "There's a good coffee bar on Lower Bridge Street."

"After we've had our walk maybe . . . somewhere down by the Cathedral. Now how can I help you, Carl?"

"I was wondering if you could look into something?" And Power told Lynch about the Inquest into Dr McAdams. How

Dr McAdams had been found dead washed up on the shore; about the abandoned boat found drifting; about the post-mortem and the overdose; about the lack of any history of depression or alcohol misuse in Dr McAdams's notes and about the strange Inquest where Power, and to a certain extent the Coroner, had been put under such pressure to judge the death a suicide.

"And," said Lynch, as they started climbing the Wishing Steps, "your intuition is that this is no suicide."

"I agree that it has been made to look like a suicide, and it is difficult to argue that its not, but I do, as you say, have a strong intuition that Dr McAdams was not ill. Stressed maybe. But not ill enough to take his own life."

Lynch stopped on the Wall between Barnaby's Tower and Newgate and briefly looked out over the remains of a Roman courtyard and gardens. He could have reeled off several reasons why Carl Power should treat his own intuition with a healthy dose of scepticism, and why for various logistical reasons Superintendent Lynch was not the right person to approach, but Carl was his friend, and he knew Power's intuitions of old, and he had never known Carl be wrong. And so Lynch did not tell Power to swallow down his suspicions and forget it all.

"How can I help, Carl?" he asked.

"I am going to talk to Dr McAdams' sister," said Power. The Coroner got the company to admit that McAdams worked with a team and that the team no longer worked together. I would like to talk to the other members of the team . . . I want to find out from his sister what kind of a man Dr McAdams was. If you can find me the other members of his team . . . I will talk to them about how he was."

"What was McAdams working on?"

Power shrugged, "I don't know. They never said." They began walking again towards Newgate and on to Thimbleby's Tower. "Can you find out about the team?"

"If you think it's important, I will," said Lynch.

"And the boat," said Power, as they crossed Eastgate and on to the Kaleyard Gate. "The boat would be important too. Where is it moored? Can we search it?" Lynch nodded. He paused to make two notes in a pocketbook.

"I will find it," Lynch said confidently. And now they were at Northgate. A flight of steps led down to the road to the Cathedral. Lynch looked at his watch. Various cafés beckoned them. "Just in time for tea," said Lynch. "I'm buying."

Together the friends clambered down the steps and into Northgate Street.

* * *

Lynch parked his car on the sea front at West Kirby, a seaside village at the tip of the Wirral peninsula. The noonday sun was high in the sky and the seagulls whirled around above in the blue. In the distance, he could see the green North Wales coast, and in the far distance, mountains crowned by cloud. The glittering tide was in. Across the water of the Dee Estuary, was tiny Hilbre Island where McAdams's boat had drifted onshore.

Lynch made his way along the promenade and crossed over to the entrance of the Sailing Club where the boat was still being held temporarily. He made his way to the crisp white main building and under a blue and gold sign found an arrow pointing to the reception area. An elderly gentleman with white hair and small blue eyes who was manning the reception desk watched Lynch unsmilingly as he came through the double doors. He stood up. "Are you here for the funeral?" he asked. "The private function?"

"Good afternoon," said Lynch. "No, no I'm not here for that."

"Well, I'm sorry the bar's closed then. The private function you see."

"My name is Superintendent Lynch of the Cheshire Constabulary. I am here on official business. Can you help me, please?" He showed his warrant card.

"Oh yes, Sir, how can I help?"

"There is a boat you are kindly keeping here for us. A boat that was found drifting."

"Oh yes, quite a mystery that. There's been a lot of interest in that boat; we've all had a look." Lynch groaned internally, if the boat was a crime scene it was now a compromised crime scene. "And the local police too. And the press too after the body was found."

Lynch wondered whether there was now the slightest point in his taking a look. "What can you tell me about the boat?"

"It's a 1990 Seamaster "Norther". Just the sort for

pottering around the coast here. Two engines, maximum 10 knots. Two cabins. Nothing special. You wouldn't want to cross any oceans in it. But okay for pottering. Do you want to see it?"

"Yes please," said Lynch.

"I can give you the keys and point you in the right direction, but I can't leave the desk unmanned. We've got funeral people coming from a memorial service at St. Bridget's."

"I'm sure I can manage, thank you for your help," said Lynch, relieved that he wouldn't have to be watched as he searched the boat.

In possession of the keys to the cabin and with direction from the old man, Lynch set off across the boatyard.

The Seamaster was a well-kept white boat with a blue canvas sprayhood covering its rear cockpit and a grey, inflatable dinghy dangling from the stern by davits. Lynch climbed aboard and went through the sprayhood into the cockpit where the captain's chair and helm were. From the grumpy old man at the desk, he had learned that any number of people had been on board after the boat had been salvaged from the sea. Nevertheless he donned thin elasticated plastic overshoes and PVC gloves from his suit pocket as a matter of habit. Lynch looked over the globe-like compass, the grey screen of the navigation guide and the various dials and red buttons of the cockpit with vague interest. It meant nothing to him, but he could see nothing awry.

He went down through the companionway into the galley

and dining area. There were breadcrumbs on the counter and paperwork strewn across the benches and the main table of the saloon. Some cushions that should have been on the foam-covered benches, were scattered on the floor. Lynch thought how he could be looking at the aftermath of a fight, or was this merely the result of the boat being tossed about on the open sea.

The fridge had some old milk and butter still in it. He looked at the 'use by' dates. The milk was four weeks out of date and separated into layers of slime and whey. The plastic of the bottle was taut with gas. The butter was still in date, just. There were some unopened cans of Heinz tomato soup and Spam in the cupboards.

He went on through to the forward cabin. A triangular bed area was let into the bow part of the hull. A sleeping area was made up. On the white cotton covered foam cushions that made up the mattress was a lonely sleeping bag, rumpled up like a caterpillar's discarded skin. Dr McAdams must have slept here when the boat was at anchor. A neat pile of books and papers lay by the two pillows. The pillows were indented where McAdams had laid his head. Lynch sat down and reached over to the books. One was *Migrants and Malaria* by Prothero. Another was an unbound proof copy of the history of malaria by Porter. The papers were handwritten. One page just said 'Finish paper!' as a memo from McAdams to himself. Another said, 'Revise.doc.' Lynch was a computer Luddite, but he knew that a .doc name suggested there was a computer file.

Lynch made his way aft and into the rear cabin. Here was

a good-sized bunk bed, covered with blankets and red striped pillows. The cabin was clean. No-one had slept here recently. A few books, ancient paperback novels by Hemingway, Steinbeck and Agatha Christie sat neatly stacked on a shelf.

He went back into the saloon area and surveyed the scattered mess that was there and concluded that if books and papers could stay in place in the two cabins, that there was more than a possibility that there had been a commotion in the saloon. He guessed that he was looking at a fight scene. With fresh eyes, he surveyed the cabin. He moved onto the saloon benches and looked at the table from a new angle, and he saw it. On the edge of a cupboard by the table was a ruddy-brown smear. He moved closer to inspect it. Blood and some hair. Somebody's face and head had impacted here. And now he looked at it, there was another smear of blood on a cupboard front near the floor.

He pulled out a mobile phone and made a call.

Then Lynch started ferreting about in every room, looking for hidden compartments, anywhere that McAdams might have hidden something. In the end he found it in the forward cabin, slid underneath the cushions of the mattress. "Hardly hidden at all," thought Lynch.

As he made his way out of the boat, carrying McAdams's laptop, Lynch looked about the crime scene. He reasoned that the crime scene had been almost forensically worthless before he'd ever stepped on board. Hundreds of fingerprints from curious people at the sailing club, their shed hairs, DNA traces and so on would have obscured the picture. If any assailant had attacked McAdams (assuming McAdams hadn't just fallen and split his head) they had missed the laptop and there would be no prints on it.

Lynch disembarked and made his way to the reception area to tell them that a scene of crime officer would be attending to take samples from the blood and hair on the boat. He wanted to warn the sailing club staff not to enter the boat until then.

Then he returned to the car with the laptop and although he was aware of normal procedures he was wondering whether to bypass protocol this once.

* * *

Dr Power parked by the side of the road, took out his notebook and checked the address of McAdams's sister, Sarah Ferguson. He got out of the Saab and brushed himself down. Flakes of pastry from a meat and potato pie that he had hastily consumed on the journey fell from his clothes as he tried to make himself more presentable. His stomach had been rumbling through his morning clinic, and he only had an hour or so before his afternoon ward round.

The houses on the street were set back from the road, buffered from traffic by short gardens defended by box hedges and occasionally bedecked by trellises of purple sweet peas or columns of red and pink hollyhocks.

Power knocked at a glossy blue front door, which was opened promptly by McAdams's brother-in-law. He looked at

Power with, what Power took to be, a curious mixture of anger and fear. "Yes?" he demanded.

"Dr Power," he offered his hand to shake, but this was seemingly puzzling to the other who ignored the gesture. Power thought an explanation might assist. "My secretary, Laura, phoned and asked if I might visit." Blankness. "I was at the Inquest of your brother-in-law, Dr McAdams . . . may I come in?"

"I know who you are," said Mr Ferguson. There was no welcome in his voice, no offer of entrance to the small house, and no sign of McAdams's sister herself. "I'm sorry Dr Power, but you've had a wasted journey. We don't want to talk to you. Would you go, please?"

"I just wanted to talk for five minutes, I wouldn't stay long."

The door closed on him, inexorably and firmly.

Of course, it was not the first time that Power had faced this sort of situation. A closed and unyielding front door often greeted attempts to visit psychotic patients when called in by a distressed family's request. Such patients might lack insight, and be paranoid that Power was in league with the devil or the KGB and both verbally or physically aggressive. In such difficult times, Power might be accompanied by an approved social worker or the police, and where Power's words of persuasion failed, there might be recourse to the Mental Health Act of 1983. In this circumstance, today, standing alone with only the hot July sun at his back, Power had no answer to the robust and silent front door.

He stepped back onto the path and wondered what to do. If Mrs Ferguson did not wish to speak to him, there was nothing to be done. Strange though, that Laura had evidently reached an agreement for Power to talk with Sarah Ferguson only that morning and by early afternoon the agreement had vapourised. The husband had looked annoyed to see Power, but also there was a smouldering anxiety evident in the widening of his eyes.

Power chanced to look up. Maybe he felt that he was being watched. At the landing window was a male figure. The figure upstairs registered Power's looking up at him and moved backwards into the shadows.

A glimpse had been enough though, certainly sufficient for Power to see that this was not Sarah's husband, but instead Power had seen the thin face of the lawyer, Cousins, looking down upon him like a Raven from the Tower.

THREE

"Come on up," Michael buzzed the door open for his younger brother, Jared.

Jared muttered to himself about always having to visit his older brother and never being visited by him.

"I can still hear you!" said his brother through the door phone panel as his brother opened the front door. He stood for a moment on the threshold of the old family home, the mansion on East 63rd Street. Behind him was the busy clatter of the street. On the right was the lush greenery of Central Park. Then he was inside the vestibule, the door was shut behind him and he was in the densely carpeted peacefulness of the hallway. Memories of childhood came flooding back to him. His nanny teaching him to walk down the stairs which stood ahead of him. Sitting to attention at breakfast in the dining room as his father finished the *New York Times,* while the help cleared away dishes of scrambled egg and toast. His mother sipping coffee and glaring at the back of the newspaper. A governess teaching him to read in the playroom. Being escorted out of the front door to Allen-Stevenson School. Years later, sitting on a trunk in the hall waiting to go back to board at Exeter, following in the footsteps of older brother Michael – and father, of course. Always following.

Jared suppressed the memories as best he could and

gathered his thoughts for the meeting ahead. He began to sweat, not because of any overwhelming anxiety, but because of the sweltering heat of what was now his brother's home. Michael had spent over twenty years in Africa, and now he tended to feel cold - even in the baking heat of a New York summer and generally had his house at least four degrees hotter - even in June.

Both sons came from the monied Howarth-Weaver family. For three generations the family had retained the controlling interest and the vast bulk of shares in what had grown from a small pharmaceutical store in New York in eighteen ninety-eight, to a multinational conglomerate, with companies delivering logistics, pharmaceuticals, agrochemicals and nutrition products worldwide.

Their sister Marianne, the eldest child, nominally chaired the parent company, which had moved to Canada in the nineteen-fifties to take advantage of a specially engineered tax deal. She was polite, demure and had the advantage of a first-class education. She had, rather unusually for the time, always been coached by their father to take over the corporation after his death. She preferred to live and work in Toronto on the opposite side of Lake Ontario to the state of New York.

Michael stuck to the old family mansion in New York. The brothers saw little of her and placed little value on her lonely contribution at the helm, always trying to maintain the corporation's delicate balances. The brothers' network of company men and their combination of shares ensured that final control always resided with them.

Jared climbed the deeply carpeted stairs up to the first floor where his older brother had created a self-contained space that he rarely left nowadays except to visit the occasional restaurant or art show. He pushed open the swing door on the landing to enter. The temperature went up a notch inside the doorway, and Jared gasped, took off his jacket and loosened his tie.

His brother Michael had not deigned to get up to come and welcome him, but was sitting in his study with a cafetiere of coffee and surrounded by three flickering computer screens displaying the world stock exchanges that were currently open.

He pointed Jared to the drinks cabinet and then waved his brother to sit down.

Jared placed a glass with ice cubes in and a bottle of twenty-five-year-old Laphroaig on the scant space that had been left available to him on Michael's desk. Michael was surrounded by books and current journals on infectious diseases and pharmacology.

"How goes it?" asked Michael, eyes still on the screens.

"I saw Marianne in England."

"Oh," said Michael raising an eyebrow. "What was she doing there?"

"Endowing a chair at the University of Allminster. Dining with Vice Chancellors and their ilk. Part of her Howarth-Weaver Foundation business."

"Very nice," Michael said flatly. "Well, they say charity covers a multitude of sins. She swans about spending the profits while we do all the dirty work. She should try getting her hands dirty for a while. Is she well?"

"She looked fine," said Jared.

"A pity," said Michael. He looked at his brother's frowning response. "Don't give me that look. Don't pretend any brotherly love towards her. There's bad blood between you and her as well. We'd both be better off without her. Oh, stop looking at me like that." Michael poured coffee for himself. "There's no need to pretend. We're of a certain age. Father's not here to berate us about what we think. We no longer have to tread on eggshells to stop Mother's moods." He sighed. Jared was silent. "I know what you think about her."

"Do you really?" Jared said quietly.

Michael judged it was time to change the subject. "I've been reading this lot," Michael waved towards the books and journals. "Waiting for you to come back and report from Europe on Project Malaria. God, these books are dry. I know more about the parasite Plasmodium falciparum and female Anopheles mosquitoes than I ever thought I would need to."

"Then you will know that the potential insecticide business is worth billions to us."

"Oh, I gathered that long ago. In the nineteen-fifties and nineteen-sixties the US alone spent $1.2billion on di chloro-diphenyl . . . tri . . ."

"Di chloro-diphenyl – tri chloroethane . . . DDT"

"Thank you, yes . . . DDT . . . to kill mosquitoes. Huge sales. Before it was banned of course."

" It's a huge market," said Jared. "Because if you go down

the insecticide route . . . it controls the malaria by killing the mosquitoes that carry the *Plasmodium* . . . you spray a wall and the mosquito dies when it lands on it . . . and you impregnate things like the sleeping nets . . . it works well, but it wears off . . . so you have to keep re-spraying walls and standing water . . . so you sell it once, then a few months later you sell more again . . . the potential recurrent sales are astronomical."

"Well, yes, we agreed that strategy last year when the Spanish team developed the new agent. And have we got the low toxicity we needed? We're not going kill off birds and cause a Silent Spring like DDT did before the ban or kill off the bloody bees, heaven forbid?"

"No," it's very safe, very unique and very, very patented in Howarth-Weaver's favour. The only downside for people is that re-spraying has to be every three months. It ceases to be active after that and wouldn't kill a fly . . . or a mosquito. But that's actually a plus for us, because obviously more frequent spraying means more sales."

"Did you tell Marianne, about the discovery?" asked Michael.

"She was delighted and keen for it to go into production as soon as possible."

"Well, aren't we pleased she's pleased . . . you didn't mention the rest of Project Malaria to her?"

Jared glared at him. "Do you think I am that stupid?"

"My apologies," said Michael. "Well, are we ready to manufacture the necessary quantities to meet demand?"

"It will take a while to gear up to the demand as the

requirements grow, but it's feasible," said Jared. " The factory in Madrid is on standby for the marketing launch next month. If there is a lag between the production and the demand, then it gives our product a premium."

"Good," said Michael. "So we are ready with the solution. And the second part of Project Malaria. The demand side? Or creating the problem for our solution?"

"Cousins has six operatives in play; they've travelled to Africa – the Democratic Republic of Congo and Chad, Brazil and Costa Rica and Myanmar. All in place in mobile labs. They will start releasing this month."

Michael nodded. "And their labs are non traceable."

"It's all at arms length . . . well it's like a chain. Cousins is pretty sure that each link is at arms length from the other link. Organised in cells . . . you know so each person in a cell only knows the people in that cell . . ."

"I know how cells work . . . you said Cousins is 'pretty sure' . . . that's not sure enough in my book. This can never be traced back to us."

"It won't, the new hardy *Anopheles* strain has been bred by a subsidiary or a subsidiary of an entirely different sleeper company in Argentina. The new treatment resistant strain of *Plasmodium* has been bred in the Philippines in a fake University lab in a village in the middle of nowhere. The funding is untraceable. Cash, filtered and transferred by courier over land. And the combination of the new, hardy mosquitoes and the new treatment resistant *Plasmodium* is being done onsite in mobile labs in the back of lorries bought with cash in different countries. It can't be traced back. And the new combinations will be released very shortly. The combination of mosquitoes and *Plasmodium* will deliver the new malaria cases within a few weeks."

"And our insecticide will come on stream at the right time. I love it when a plan comes together, Jared."

Jared nodded. "And the demand will be fierce. The new mosquitoes are hardy . . . they can exist many miles north and south of the equatorial regions – the traditional malaria zones. And the *Plasmodium* itself is not sensitive to traditional drugs . . . so the only solution is prevention . . . with our sprays."

Michael was watching the markets on the screens . . . shares were dipping in the Far East, just as he had thought they would. "And it would have been a perfect business plan too, except for the irony . . . how is that unfinished business in England?"

The irony was the unforeseen consequence of a large conglomerate. As the brothers had been developing their plans to market a new Howarth-Weaver insecticide to prevent the mosquitoes that spread the disease, they had learned the unwelcome fact that another Howarth-Weaver subsidiary had been developing a new compound to treat the malaria. It was a simple case of maths projections. Five minutes with a basic spreadsheet had convinced Michael that sales of the drug would never match recurrent global sales of the insecticide.

The solution had been simple. Cousins had been dispatched.

"Well, the situation is contained," said Jared. The

unfinished business is not wholly concluded though. The progress is that the drug development team has been disbanded. The drug lab has been broken up. The compound destroyed. Records from the lab burned. The lead investigator was found dead, washed upon the shore. The Inquest managed by Cousins. Some questions. Not the preferred verdict of suicide. Some awkward questions . . . but what can they do?"

"You mentioned the drug development team . . . and I think you used the term disbanded? I think when we spoke before I used the term 'elimination'. I think that is still the preferred arrangement. We can't have any voices from beyond the grave. We can't have two solutions to our problem. Especially not when one solution – the drug – undercuts our preferred solution – the insecticide. And we can't let any voices be heard . . . so as I instructed before . . . it is elimination that is the preferred term. Don't you agree, brother?"

"Well yes, I suppose I do," said Jared.

"Well, I only I hope Cousins is up to it," said Michael. "For your sake."

FOUR

Dr Power looked at the young man in front of him called Adam. He smiled brightly, and his face was the very picture of ruddy good health. And yet here he was the focus of Power's regular ward round, sitting in an armchair in the centre of the room, with a ring of professionals around him. Sam, the occupational therapist, smiling as ever; Jane the ward sister, scribbling notes in her Kardex files and munching a chocolate cookie surreptitiously; Kylie, a student nurse from the University of Chester and Dr Power's junior doctor, Rachel.

Before Adam had entered, Rachel had outlined his history. A high-flying twenty-six-year-old IT consultant from an International firm of management specialists. He had been found wandering in the city centre, oblivious of traffic, penniless, shoeless and at first unable to remember his name. He had not been drunk and not been taking drugs. His blood and urine screens were clear. His fiancée gave a history that he had walked out of their brand new flat to get some bacon, bread, and milk and not come back. Rachel said that she had found nothing wrong with him when she interviewed him.

"And the police picked you up?" asked Power.

"Absolutely," Adam said brightly. As Power looked at him he was checking his mood, which seemed normal, although perhaps blandly unconcerned with his circumstances.

Admission to a psychiatric unit is not an everyday occurrence. His pupils seemed neither constricted nor dilated. He was not sweating. So drug or alcohol problems seemed unlikely explanations for his wandering. "Will I be here long?" asked Adam.

"Where do you think you should be?" Power expected Adam to mention his work. It was Monday morning after all.

"At a wedding. My friend is getting married. I'm the best man."

"Oh," said Power, following the train of thought on instinct. "Is that right? What's his name?"

"Giles. Works with me at Price's."

"Have you got your Best Man's speech ready?" asked Power.

"Yes, it's here!" He pulled a sheaf of papers from his jacket pocket and gave it to Power. Carl glanced at it. The speech was word-processed. He could see Giles's name. The speech seemed genuine.

"It looks great," said Power smiling. He looked at Rachel the junior doctor and frowned at her. "What date is the wedding?"

For the first time Adam looked perplexed. "I don't know. It's slipped my mind."

"Could it be today?"

"I suppose it could be," said Adam.

Power looked at Rachel again and asked, "Do you remember who I am, Adam? My name?"

"No," said Adam. "I don't think we've been introduced."

"And the place we're in Adam, what's the name of this place where we are?"

Adam looked around the ward round room for clues. "A hospital?"

"Okay Adam, I need to talk to the staff here. I wonder if you could wait outside and my junior doctor will come and see you. Before you go, is there anything at all that you want to ask me, or tell me?"

Adam shook his head but smiled in a most unconcerned manner. He stood up, and a little unsteadily for a young man, walked from the room.

The ward sister escorted him from the room and Power turned to his junior. He was polite to Rachel, but she could tell that he was angry. He asked her, "What are you thinking of doing now?"

"Er . . . a full cognitive examination, and tests."

Power nodded. "Please can you go and do that now while I finish off the ward round? Make sure you arrange an urgent CT scan and an EEG."

When Rachel had left to examine Adam properly, and Jane had returned, the ward sister asked Power what he thought. "I didn't know why Adam had been admitted, at first," he said.

"I know, we were wondering that too. He seems so nice."

"Mmm," said Power. "He was completely unconcerned he'd been admitted. Rather incongruous. His gait is slightly unsteady. He is disorientated and his memory for details he would know – like the date of his friend's wedding – is abnormally poor. He is dementing."

"How can you say that? He's so young!" said Jane. "You can't be sure."

"You're quite right. I can't be sure. We need to await test results. Until we get the results can you make sure he eats in his room, has his own cutlery, plates and cups. And that nurses know to keep clear of any . . . Er . . . bodily fluids . . . and to keep any fluids away from the other patients." He looked at Jane, who was regarding him with an open mouth. "I will explain after," he said. "It's a precaution."

* * *

Several days had passed since Dr Power's last ward round. Desperate to please her consultant, Rachel, the junior doctor on Power's team, had almost moved the moon and the stars themselves in trying to get the tests that he had requested. Armed with the results and having worked up the case into a fine academic exercise she was prepared to expound for hours if need be.

Disappointingly for her however Power seemed not to want to be impressed by her exposition, but wanted to focus on specifics. He had spotted Adam, his fiancée and his father outside the ward round room as he came in after lunch, and he was unusually nervous.

"So," he said, as the team discussed the case with the patient and family outside. "He remains the same? Disorientated?"

"Yes."

"Forgetful?"

"Yes."

"And he doesn't protest that he wants to leave? He seems quite happy?"

"Blissfully unconcerned." Power's frown deepened.

"And you've spoken to the family? When did they first notice any change?"

"His fiancée thought he'd been stressed. He seemed absent-minded.

"Please . . . I asked when they noticed."

"His fiancée says a month, his father says he's been 'different' - not worried - he's usually worried about everything - for a couple of months."

"Nothing on the CT scan?" Rachel shook her head. "And the EEG . . . It showed abnormal activity didn't it? Slow waves and sharp complexes?"

Rachel read the report that had been typed that very morning and which she had gone to the labs specially to pick up for Power. It was as if Power had read it already. "It says 'diffuse slowing and frontal rhythmic delta activity and periodic sharp wave complexes."

Power slumped in his seat. He sighed. With his elbows on the arms of the chair, he steepled his hands together and deep in thought, put his fingers to his lips, staring into the middle distance. He eventually looked up at Rachel. "How old is he again?"

"Twenty-six."

"Damn it. He had everything in front of him," said Power.

"A career. A wife. Decades of potential." He looked at Rachel and the ward sister. "This is going to be difficult. Psychiatry isn't usually life and death stuff, although it can sometimes be, most of the time it's not. We need to send Adam to have more specialist tests. But I'm pretty sure this is Creutzfeldt-Jakob disease. A prion dementia."

"He's too young," protested Jane.

"I wish that I was wrong," said Power. "But I'm sorry that I'm not. There have been cases in *The Lancet* of a 16-year-old and an 18-year-old with this. It will be very rapid. He has maybe six months or so." The staff gaped at Power. "It needs checking with the neurologists, before we can confirm anything at all to them. But I need to see them now, just them and me alone. To prepare the way for all this." He seemed to sag in the chair and to diminish. "Please can we clear the room, Sister? And then please can you ask them to come in? I'll take it from there."

* * *

Power was called down to the ward as an emergency at 5.30 p.m. The nurses had a difficult young man in the seclusion room, one of the other consultants' patients who had only been admitted earlier that day, after trying to burn his mother alive in her bed. The only four nurses available had a limb each and, as a result, the rest of the ward was abandoned. Patients milled about, largely good-naturedly as Power keyed himself onto the acute ward and hurried down the ward corridor towards the seclusion room at the end. A manic female made ribald remarks about getting into his pants as he hurried past. Another psychotic male patient twirled a sock with a snooker ball in around his head and leered at Power, "Shall I knock your fucking block off, mate?" Strangely Power felt no fear of, or anger towards, the genuinely ill.

He found the few nurses that were on duty and the patient on the floor in a seething, writhing mass of arms and legs. The patient was screaming about being abused, but was highly aroused and muttering about devils flying in the air above his head. Behind Power, the man with the sock-cosh was shouting to 'Leave my mate alone! Get off him or I'll stove your fucking heads in."

Power turned and asked him politely to give him the sock and to return to his room like a reasonable person.

"Okay, Dr Power," he said meekly and handing the sock over, headed off.

"Carl, can you help?" asked the charge nurse, Terry, on the seclusion room floor and trying to hold the patient's arm and shoulder as the patient bucked and heaved.

"We need a stat injection of levompromazine - 100mg im and 4mg of lorazepam - someone go and draw it up." Power looked at the female staff nurse wrestling with the patient's leg. "I'll replace you," he offered. He got hold of the patient's leg to enable her to move away and draw the sedation up. "Go on, quickly," he said. "I'll write it up when you come back." The patient's body was thrusting and bucking like a wild bronco, with superhuman strength. The patient was on his back because patients restrained on their front are at risk of breathing difficulties and may die. Power found it difficult to hold down just the one leg he was managing.

Four staff members are rarely enough to restrain a violent, fully grown psychotic human male. On the ward that night there was one adult staff member, including the doctor, to each limb. But that left the patient's head free. Power cried out a warning, but with horror he saw the patient's head moving towards the charge nurse's arm. "Look out for his teeth," Power cried, but the charge nurse had little option over what to do. To move out of the way and abandon the patient to his own devices, or to let go his arm and thereby endanger other staff. The charge nurse chose to hang on, to protect his staff and the doctor, and to take the consequences of his altruism.

Power watched in absolute horror as the patient sank his teeth into the charge nurse's arm. He saw the nurse's masklike face of pain, the teeth clamping on his skin, sinking into the elasticity of the epidermis. The skin held for a moment under the pressure and then gave way, and the incisors bit deep until the blood flowed. Laughing manically, the patient chewed down the flesh. Power cried out, "The injection! Quickly!" And the female staff nurse was back and the twin syringes – one of levomepromazine and one of lorazepam were plunged deep into the patient's quadriceps muscle – the best large muscle available. It took maybe four minutes for the lorazepam to circulate properly, and for the patient's body to slacken and to slump unconscious.

Power quickly assessed the man's pulse and breathing. "Put him in the recovery position and let's get out."

Power and the less senior nurses led the way out of the seclusion room, while the damaged charge nurse checked his patient one last time and retreated, clutching his arm, still pumping fresh blood from the bite wound. He locked the door and made his way towards the office to write up the note. "Stop," said Power, "what are you doing? Get to A&E now." He turned to the staff nurse. "Go with him, please."

"Who'll man the ward?" asked the charge nurse. He was pale.

"I will,' said Power. "I'll phone for your replacement. Go on. You can't stay – get well."

Power watched as the charge nurse was led away, and turned to the phones to summon extra help. As he listened to the ringing tones, he automatically began writing up the prescription and searched out the patient's record to document the incident.

That night he drove home past the old psychiatric hospital, now closed. Lights were on in the building as contractors were working through the night, turning the complex into prestige apartments for profit. He muttered something about money and corruption and switched on the radio of his classic Saab, wound down the car window and turned up the music as high as it could go.

* * *

Power met Lynch for Saturday lunch at the Rams Head in Disley. They sat in comfy chairs near a pointed stone archway and scanned the menu over two pints of bitter. "I think I'll have the roast beef," said Lynch. He looked up at Power. "Why do you frown? You like beef don't you?"

"I did," said Power. "But I've been having second and third thoughts."

"What do you mean?"

"A patient," said Power. "A young man in his twenties has developed dementia. And the culprit, as far as I can make out is meat, beef. The BSE outbreak in cattle a few years back – seems to be associated with a new illness in humans. It's just that you hear the news about things, and you think these things can't affect you. You carry on just the way you've always done. But seeing him sitting there in front of me, talking to his family . . . has made me wonder whether the time has come to stop eating meat."

"I'm not sure I can avoid meat," said Lynch. "But today we could have fish if you like? I see there's some cod." Power nodded, and so they ordered that.

"I went to see the boat," said Lynch. "And I think that you are right. I don't think McAdams's death was . . . unassisted. There were signs of a struggle in the saloon area of the boat. Everywhere else on board was pristine, but things had been thrown about the saloon and galley. And there were two smears of blood. They have been analysed, and they match the dead Dr McAdams."

"What about fingerprints?" asked Power.

"The rest of the boat, as a crime scene, was compromised. I wasn't the first on board after the boat came to shore. It's not their fault. No-one knew it was a crime scene."

Lynch reached into the bag he had brought with him. "Can I trust you with this? This is McAdams's laptop."

Power reached over and took it. "Isn't it evidence?"

"I can't think of anyone more trustworthy. McAdams hid it, not very well, under a foam cushion in his cabin. But they didn't find it, I don't think. I would like you to have a look at it, but it's a puzzle."

"How so?"

"McAdams set a password. We haven't been able to crack it, and I thought you, as a doctor, might think of what it is better than I. The laptop may have nothing on it of any use. Maybe it just has a load of games on it, but have a go will you?"

With this, two plates of fish and chips arrived to accompany their beer, and their conversation turned to the food.

Later, at Alderley House, on his own, Power found an adaptor that fitted the laptop and watched as lights blinked on as he plugged it in. The fan for the motherboard inside whirred into life and Power opened the screen up.

The screen was blank except for a single word, a silent one word question, 'Password?>' which blinked at him.

He typed the obvious, the surname 'McAdams' and pressed the return key. Nothing.

He typed the obvious, the Christian name 'Fergus' and pressed the return key. Nothing.

And so he went on for the next hour, until with mounting frustration he shoved the laptop away, and went to the back door and opened it to step out into the night air. He looked up at the moon and stars and sucked the fresh air into his lungs.

FIVE

The desiccated ham sandwiches, curled and partially mummified, sat reproachfully on a platter in the centre of the boardroom table. Around the table were gathered several clinical directors from General Medicine, Surgery, and Radiology, the Chief Executive, a smattering of non-Executive Directors, the Trust Chairman, and the Commissioner of Hospital Services from the Health Authority. Power was there on sufferance, a deputy of the Mental Health Directorate. He had strict instructions from the Director to attend, but to say nothing. Nothing. Power was, and he felt, like a dummy propped up against the walls of a besieged Foreign Legion fort in the desert. Merely there for show.

His mind wandered as the table discussed a potential reorganisation of the purchasers by the new Health Secretary. He sipped a bitter lukewarm brown liquid that was masquerading as coffee. 'Just as I am masquerading on behalf of the Clinical Director,' thought Power. His meeting papers bore the acronym 'ALOOC' he had scrawled across the top. He and his secretary Laura shared the code that deciphered his various personal acronyms. ALOOC deciphered as 'A Load of Old Crap'.

The meeting had been proceeding without his notice or input for over an hour. It was a warm day. It was sunny outside. Power was day-dreaming. Some words however began to percolate through the haze of Power's boredom. "Our staffing levels are the best they have ever been," the Chief Executive was saying. "We have more consultants and nurses than ever before."

"But that's because we've merged several units." Power was surprised to find he had spoken and that the words he had just listened to, had actually been his own. Everybody was looking at him. The Chief Executive was glaring at him, nostrils actually flaring. "Erm . . . we are actually quite short of nurses in psychiatry".

"Are you really, Dr Power?" said Mrs Simons, the new Chief Executive. "Psychiatry actually reported a financial surplus last month. Perhaps you should speak to your Clinical Director if you have a problem."

"We ran short of funds in Medicine last month," the gimlet-eyed Dr Archer announced. "If psychiatry achieved a surplus, perhaps it could be vired over to our budget?"

Dr Archer's intervention prompted the Chief Executive to look smugly at Power as if to warn him that his few brief sentences during the meeting could effectively reduce the psychiatry budget. Unable to suppress his desire to explain, Power went bravely on, "We are short of nursing staff. I was called on to the ward on Tuesday night. Only two trained staff and a student. They had to restrain a violent male patient and try and get him into seclusion. I'm not sure if you have been in such a situation? You need four to six staff trained in control and restraint – otherwise it's dangerous for the patient and the staff. I had to physically assist. A big struggle. The charge nurse had his arm bitten through. Bitten through – in front of me. That's how I know that there is a nurse shortage."

The Health Authority representative looked at Power rather as if he smelt. Mrs Simons's face was a stony mask. "These kind of arguments Dr Power . . . are merely medical shroud waving – we're used to them and to be frank, they hold little water with experienced committees. I suggest, again, that you take this clinical issue to the Clinical Director. This is not the correct venue for such clinical detail."

"But, Mrs Simons, this is a Hospital Board meeting," said Power, oblivious of the clear political message the Chief Executive was sending him. The Health Authority representative and the non-Executives looked uncomfortable. They were usually spared such unpleasant detail. Violent patients. Nurses with injuries. Power battled on to the committee's further discomfort. "If this isn't the place to discuss urgent clinical shortages, where is?"

The Chief Executive snapped through pursed lips, "Let's move to a discussion on our Clinical Governance priorities, shall we? Agenda, Item 5"

Afterwards, over another nondescript coffee, Power stood alone as the hospital directors clustered and chatted. A mousy looking lady sidled up to Power. She introduced herself as Mary, a non-Executive of the hospital, and asked whether what Power had said was true, and if so, how was the poor nurse. Power saw a faint glimmer of sympathy for the victim. "He's off work.'" said Power. "I'm not sure he'll be back".

You mean he'll move to a competing Trust?"

"No," said Power, "I mean that these kind of assaults often mean the end of a career".

* * *

Power looked over the top of his copy of *The Guardian* towards the hospital corridor where the noise was coming from. Abruptly, his secretary, Laura, poked her head round the door and hissed at him, "Hide! The Chief Executive's down the corridor. I don't think she's very happy with you."

Power frowned. A brief twinge of fear gripped him. Then he steadied himself. "I've not done anything wrong." He said out loud, and his remark was as much to comfort himself as to reassure his secretary.

"She's with the Clinical Director right now," Laura said, raising an eyebrow.

"Ah," said Power, looking around his office in a rather puzzled way. The place seemed suddenly unfamiliar territory, as if he were looking at it for the first time. "I suppose it's about the Board meeting."

"And the interview you gave," she said somewhat downcast. "You may have pushed things a bit too far this time."

"If we don't speak up," said Power. "The hospitals will all go . . . then where will my patients be?"

It was too late; the Chief Executive sailed into the office past his secretary, like a grey, shoulder-padded battleship.

"Your patients, Dr Power? I do not believe you own any

patients. I rather think that the patients you see are only seen by you because the Trust asks you to see them."

"Ah," said Power, getting to his feet in an effort to be polite. "Good afternoon, Mrs Simons. Will you sit down?"

"Is it?" The Chief Executive folded her hands behind her back and ignored his invitation to sit down. "I rather think it is not. I have just spent half an hour talking to an investigative journalist from . . ." she paused and looked at his newspaper. She continued in strident tones, speaking quickly and brooking no interruption. "That particular newspaper that you have there. She was asking very pointed questions about the Private Finance Initiative and our initiative with Beacon Mental Health Limited. Questions that would suggest she had a very good knowledge of our Trust's local affairs . . . of what I consider to be our private corporate business, Dr Power".

"If it's about the Board meeting I was just trying to point out that maybe it's not such a good deal for the Health Service . . . it will saddle us with debt for years to come . . . all that interest to be paid . . . a phenomenal rate . . . surely it must impact on services for future years."

"Do I tell you what to prescribe for your patients? Do you have any qualifications in business, Dr Power?"

"No, but anyone can see that signing up to this system will transfer vast amounts of public money into the private sector."

"This is Labour Government policy, Dr Power, it's nothing unusual. It's not controversial. It's happening all across the land. Why you should make waves about our Trust . . . it's not helpful."

"I feel like the boy who points out that the Emperor is wearing no clothes . . . it doesn't matter what people say to him or about him or what happens to him. The Emperor is still naked."

Mrs Simons sighed. "Why can't you conform, Dr Power? Why can't you fit in?"

Dr Power stood up. "Because your staff are not components that can be fitted in, or replaced when they are unpredictable, or when they are simply being human. Because our patients are not playing a game called 'business' with profit and loss and winners and losers. Because patients have no choice, but to be patients and it's our privilege to be in a temporary position where we can help them. And, inevitably, when we ourselves fall ill; when we grow old, then we can only hope that we will receive the help we ourselves need in turn. Because that's the reality of life. And not some self-aggrandising game."

"What are you saying?"

Power had reached the door. "I'm resigning. Because I have free will."

She waited until he was in the corridor and called out to him. "Can I have that in writing by tomorrow, Dr Power?"

As she listened to his receding footsteps, she allowed herself a self-congratulatory smile of triumph. One less troublemaker.

* * *

Power slumped onto the sofa in a crumpled and dejected state. He put his head in his hands and groaned out loud, but there was no-one to hear. A flurry of unpleasant thoughts bedevilled him. How could he cope without a salary? Would he ever find another steady consultant post or would he be consigned to the world of shifting, short-lived itinerant locum posts, each well paid admittedly, but rootless. How could he have been so impulsive? What to do now?

He stood up to go and do something, but realised he had no idea what he wanted to do. Sat down. Stood up again and indecisively mused whether he was hungry. He decided that the crisis of the day had killed his appetite stone dead. His mind raced.

How to quiet it? Exercise? A walk, a long walk such as Charles Dickens used to take – ranging over the night-time drizzle wet pavements, through the narrow streets of Victorian London. Far removed from the leafy roads of Alderley Edge and the new mansions built by overly cash-stuffed football players. Still, if he was physically tired, maybe his mind might quieten and allow him some sleep.

He pulled on a coat and changed into walking shoes. As the front door swung open, the evening air was fresh upon his face, and he was grateful for the breeze and even the misty speckles of rain that blew into his thought-fevered face.

He didn't know how or where he walked, far over the escarpment and through lanes and fields, but eventually after a few hours or so he found himself in the centre of the village, just a few miles from home. He contemplated buying a pint of bitter, but in a puritanical vein of thought judged that he should avoid alcohol to cope.

He sat down under a tree and pulled out a mobile phone. The Nokia was one of the first he had ever owned and in those days such a phone was still a marvel to him. He found a weak but just present signal and pressed out a number.

Lynch answered, "Good evening, Lynch here."

"It's Carl. Can you talk?"

"Of course," Lynch heard the uncharacteristic note of anxiety in his friend's voice. "Is everything all right?"

"Not really," and Power related the trials of the last few days. And in doing so, in talking it out with Lynch, he realised that he had felt alienated from his employers at the hospital for months, not days.

At the end of it all Lynch paused and sighed. "Well, Carl, you are a doctor, your professional knowledge and skills are all still there, and as people always say, as one door closes another opens. And, if you will forgive me, the wisdom in the Bible tells us that 'whosever shall not receive you, nor hear your words, when ye depart out of that house or city, shake off the dust of your feet.'" He paused. Power imagined Lynch by his open fireside, sipping a mug of strong tea. "And of course, the Lord always provides. So something will turn up. Does that help?"

"Yes, yes it does. It's good to hear your voice, to talk it through."

"I am always here. Come round anytime you like."

Power finished the call and closed the phone up. His

attention returned to his surroundings, and he suddenly realised that someone was sitting by his side. How long had he been there? "I'm sorry," said Power, looking at the stranger. "I didn't see you."

"We've met before," the man said.

Power looked him over. The stranger was slightly unkempt, but he wasn't a patient that Power recognised. His voice was educated, calm, precise, but warm. His long hair and beard were unfashionable. A green knapsack or bundle sat at his feet.

"Are you the Piper?"

"You remember me? I was a Piper, and I will be again I dare say. We met on the Edge, in the woods."

"Yes, yes, we did."

"Is everything all right with you?" The Piper's eyes were blue, unblinking, kind.

"I'm less certain than I was when we first met," said Power. "A lot has happened."

The Piper nodded. "I know. And we both have far to go. You have to travel soon, I think. And you will be restless for a good while, I guess. Sometimes it does feel like everything is clouded in unknowing. Well, maybe you will only rest when you go beyond that cloud and find God is or God is not . . ." Power frowned. He remembered the sense of perplexity he had felt before when he met this man. And yet he didn't think the man was unwell. The Piper seemed utterly sincere.

"And what will you do?" asked Power, trying to shift the man and the focus of his eyes and speech away from himself.

"Ah, well we both have some bad blood to sort out, it seems." Mine is closer to home than yours. Some work to do with my Father, yet. Your work lies abroad."

"But I wouldn't take work abroad. I'd only seek employment as a doctor in this country."

The Piper looked up at the darkening sky. "You've got time to walk up the hill and home before it pours, if you start now." He rummaged in a pocket and brought out a recorder and tootled a few notes. "I'll sit here a while." After a further phrase of music, the Piper stopped and mused for a moment, then smiled, "The important work we do in life is not always work."

"What is your name? I never ask."

"And I never really say, to anyone. Not for centuries. You can call me Simon, if you like, but I'm not that Simple. Simon Harker, shall we say, maybe, for Harker was my mother's name, but what's in a name?"

At this, Power stood up, shook the Piper's hand, shook his own head in bewilderment and hurried down the High Street. Alone under the tree the Piper watched for a few minutes, then sounded out a tune, which wafted after Power on the air. The music followed Power as he walked briskly up the hill. As Power turned a corner and disappeared from view the Piper took the recorder from his lips and stowed it in his pack, picked up his own burden and walked away into the dusk.

* * *

The front door of Alderley House was a tall and stout oaken

affair, painted pale green. The door sat within a gothic stone arch. At each edge of the stone hood mould that stood out over the archway to throw off rainwater were animals shaped into label stops, a signature from the architect, Waterhouse.

Power arrived at the door out of breath from striding up the hill.

He let himself in and slammed the door behind him, grateful to have reached his home. Alone in the silence, he let out an expletive-ridden oath about the Chief Executive and instantly felt better for this.

All at once he noticed the flashing red light of the answerphone as it sat on the table under the vast hall mirror. Power pressed play.

A woman's voice, tinged with fear. "Oh . . . er . . . Dr Power? Is that you? Oh, of course, you're not there. This is Sarah. Dr McAdams's sister. I'm so sorry about what happened. When you called round, you know? I wanted to say sorry. It wasn't us. Me and my husband. We were told. Can we try again? Should we meet somewhere neutral though? Somewhere he can't find us? Phone me on my mobile." She reeled off the number, and Power knew he'd have to replay the message with a pen and paper in hand. "Help us, Dr Power. I'm frightened."

SIX

At home, Power finished the last morsel of scrambled egg and mushrooms on toast with gusto, and washed it down with strong black coffee. So far, his new diet was going well. No meat for a week now. He checked his watch. A busy day lay ahead of him.

He phoned Laura, his secretary, at the hospital. Technically Power was working his notice at the hospital. Whenever he saw Laura at work, she would not meet his eyes, would make an excuse and leave the room. Power wondered if she hated him.

She answered, "Laura, Dr Power's secretary. Can I help you?"

"It's Carl," he said. "How are things?" Silence. He had asked her to confirm arrangements with Sarah Ferguson before. "Erm . . . have you heard any cancellations from Mrs Ferguson? Is it still on?"

"Yes, of course, are you coming in later?" He assented. "Carl, while you're on the phone can I ask you – please can't you rethink what you've done? The resignation?"

"I could, but I can't carry on in the Trust when . . . is Terry back?"

"Terry?"

"The charge nurse on the ward. That Terry. The one who was bitten."

"He's off sick still. And the word is that he's not coming back," said Laura.

"Terry going off. After what happened to him. The shortage of nurses. And the Chief Executive didn't care. You could tell she didn't care. Everyone has an agenda there. But the agenda isn't about patient care or staff safety. I can't stay Laura."

"What will you do? You haven't got another post lined up have you?"

Power had been trying not to think too hard about the future. "Something will turn up, I hope."

"What you're doing is either very brave or very stupid, Carl." It sounded like she was on the verge of tears. Power felt puzzled. "I just wanted to say that . . . I'm going to miss you." She put the phone down before she could say anymore. Power frowned.

* * *

They had arranged to meet near the Orangery at a National Trust property. Power made his way there in his ancient Saab and wandered towards the ticket office past fields of watchful cattle. Some ducks and ducklings waddled across the path towards a large duck pond that was viridian in colour, and dotted with occasional white feathers. The mother duck eyed Power warily and seemed to menace him with a glare.

Power paid his admission fee at the desk and declined to purchase the guidebook for Dunham Massey or a National

Trust annual membership. He noted where the restaurant was and then wended his way through the deer park towards the walled garden.

The sky was a brilliant blue and the sun beat down on his neck. He shrugged off his jacket and slung it over his shoulder. A look at his watch indicated he was ten minutes early, and he meandered through the beds of flowers and shrubs. He occasionally looked at the labels – azaleas, hydrangeas, blue poppies, and hostas, but absolutely nothing seemed familiar, but then he was no gardener. The garden was quiet, and he wondered about returning sometime to meditate in its peace for a few hours.

The orangery was a tall, rectangular brick building with five arched windows, built in 1720. He drifted in through the doorway and mused over some surreal old photographs of the Earl of Stamford entertaining the Emperor Haile Selassie of Ethiopia to tea in the garden outside.

"Dr Power?" Suddenly there was a voice behind him, and he turned to see a small, prim looking woman dressed in a long, pale linen coat. Her bobbed hair was fair or grey. Power couldn't decide. Her eyes were blue, and she held out a small hand in greeting to shake his hand. Her voice was warm but tremulous.

"Carl Power," he replied and squeezed her hand. Power couldn't actually remember her from the Inquest as the family had seemed so much in shadow of the malign solicitor, Cousins. "I've never been here before," he said. "I like the gardens."

She nodded. "It's quiet usually. That's why I chose it. We sometimes bring a picnic and eat it in here. You can't eat in the deer park though. Horseflies all around and the deer are really inquisitive."

"Shall we get some tea maybe? Some cake?" They made their way in silence to the restaurant, which was only just opening for the morning. Power and Mrs Ferguson were the first customers. She chose an Earl Grey tea with lemon and Power helped himself to a cafetiere of black coffee, a bowl of locally grown raspberries, a raisin-filled scone, jam and clotted cream. Mrs Ferguson eyed his elevenses and wondered if Power had not eaten breakfast. She said nothing though, out of politeness. She sipped her tea and looked out of the round windows of the barn-like restaurant abstractedly. As she watched Power scoffing his scone she felt somewhat maternal towards him, although she was probably only twenty or so years older than him. He looked up at her.

"What would you like to talk about, Mrs Ferguson?"

"I almost feel that don't know what to say. With the sunlight and the atmosphere, everything seems so safe here, and everything that's happened seems a bit like a bad dream. I suppose life goes on . . ." She sighed and reached for a handkerchief and dabbed at the corners of her eyes. "I was so confused for weeks after I heard my brother had died. I felt numb. As if everything was happening to someone else. As if I was unreal. Then we were told about the inquest. And the night before he arrived on our doorstep. Unannounced."

"I'm sorry," said Power. "Who arrived?"

"Mr Cousins. He said he'd been sent by the Company Fergus worked for in order to protect us. To make sure we were looked after. He implied we were at great risk from the media or something. I never knew what. He took over. Before I knew it I'd offered a bed to him for the night. He only left a few days ago."

"He stayed with you – in your house?" asked Power, frowning.

"I didn't want him to, but I found I'd invited him and somehow I couldn't ask him to go. I didn't feel I could. He was just so very imposing, and he kept emphasising that we were in danger. Now he's gone I'm only just beginning to wake up really, to think for myself again."

"Where did he go?"

"He said he had worked abroad, for the company. He said we'd be all right, if we didn't make a fuss or talk to anybody after he went." She looked at Power's eyes. He looked an understanding man.

"Dr Power . . . it was just as if he was this dark, suffocating black bird . . . We didn't feel we could leave. My husband stopped going to work. I stopped going out to shop. Food was delivered to us by someone Cousins spoke to. He didn't let us use the telephone alone. He sat at the edge of the room. Silent. Just out of sight, listening. Do you know the weirdest thing?" Power shook his head. "He didn't sleep, or at least I think he never did."

"Why didn't you call for help?"

"Well, Dr Power, he insisted that he was the help we

needed. He just arrived one day, without warning, stayed for as long as he thought necessary and then left as suddenly. On the first night he stayed I woke up in the middle of the night. I was thirsty and thought about getting a glass of orange juice. I put on my dressing gown and left the bedroom to go downstairs. But he was sitting there. On the landing – sitting bolt upright on a dining-room chair on the landing. In that dark suit of his. His hands on his knees, staring ahead. His big black boots on. Silent. Looking ahead at me. Not a word. Not moving. Hardly breathing. I was so shocked to see him there. I went back in the bedroom and shut the door. He didn't have to tell me. And you could tell he was there outside, all the time we were asleep, or not, in our room. Every night. Just waiting." She shuddered.

"Did he ask you much, about your brother?"

"He asked, and he asked, but I didn't tell. My brother told me some stuff, but warned me that there were things I should never say to anybody who asked me."

"You are here talking to me."

"There's a difference though isn't there between the man who asks and the man who listens. That's what my brother said. That there would be someone who asked and someone who listened. And that I could tell the man who listened. That's you."

"That's me I suppose. I have to listen," said Power. "But I don't know much about your brother. I know he worked for Howarth-Weaver, a pharmaceutical company; that he did research. But that could be anything. That he had a research team. That he had some sleeping problems in the last few weeks. But I didn't get the feeling that he had a severe depression, or that he would kill himself, from his notes." She sobbed suddenly, covered her face with her handkerchief and her shoulders shook. Power reached out a hand to comfort her.

As her emotions stabilised again, she stole a look at Power and began to talk again. "Fergus had been working for years on malaria. On a cure for it. Some drug. I understand that a lot of the malaria bugs are resistant these days to the older drugs. He'd been very buoyant about his progress. He had a small team of researchers, and they were all very conscientious. Committed scientists who'd rather spend their nights and weekends in a lab or the library figuring out the answer to some research question that bothered them than enjoying themselves. Fergus was like that. He always, always put his work first. We'd see him at Christmas for a few days. He'd fulfil his family duties gladly, but he was a driven man. Dedicated. Then a few weeks before he disappeared he called round to see us. I didn't tell Cousins about any of this. I suppose I should have told the Coroner. But Cousins was there . . ."

"And he took over," said Power.

"He wouldn't let you think for yourself."

"I know what you mean," said Power. "Go on."

"Fergus called round – late at night. It was so like him. He was excited, and said his research was going so well, but he was agitated, you know, not excited in a good way. He said that his work was being closed down. He didn't agree. Couldn't understand it. And he seemed distracted. Frightened. He said he wasn't sleeping. That he'd argued with his managers. And he said his team, the three of them, were being let go. He said that he'd told them to go, not to wait around. Just go. It didn't sound right. I asked him to stop with us a few days, so that we could see he was all right; that he would settle. But he said he was all right and that he couldn't stay with us. That it was safer if he went and that he would be in touch. If we didn't hear for a few weeks it was because he was getting away from it all. His two co-workers had already gone. I knew them through Fergus. I'd met them at a scientific book launch we'd been invited to at the University. Corrine and Marcus. Cousins kept asking about them. If I knew where they were."

"Did you tell him?" asked Power, but he knew the answer. She shook her head.

"I'd die before I told Cousins that. He was compelling, but Fergus had warned me that night not to say anything about Corrine or Marcus. And my promise to Fergus stuck in my mind stronger than anything."

Power mused. Malaria meant bad air. Medical school lectures about mosquitoes with parasites in their bellies, and humans with terrible fevers and encephalitic ravings came vaguely back to him. He shuddered at the thought of the long legs and small, round, alien head of the female mosquito and its long, piercing stylet mouthparts.

"Fergus gave me this, in case I needed it. You'll know what to do with it. He arranged for them to go away . . . places for them and jobs. They went because they believed in him when he said that they had to go. Fergus said that only I had this piece of information." She reached across the table and put a small slip of paper in his hand.

Power opened it up, a long number, clearly written in red Biro. "It's a mobile number," said Power.

"Fergus wrote it down and said I should ring it only if something happened to him. The number should have reached Corrine."

"Have you tried it?"

"Over and over," she said. And her red-rimmed eyes turned liquid again. "I'm worried something's happened to her."

Power nodded determinedly. "Leave it with me. I know someone, a good man we can trust. He will help us, without fail."

"I've trusted you, Dr Power. Don't let us down. I think that I've trusted you with our lives, don't you? I can't tell you how frightened we've been."

* * *

Some weeks previously McAdams had anchored his boat just off the North Wales coast near Holyhead. He had moored in a natural harbour fringed by a curve of rock and sand. He was dog-tired, and as he was well away from any shipping lane and shore and in shallow water thought he could steal a few hours' sleep before dawn, and then he would set off across the Irish Sea to Castletown in the Isle of Man and then rest up for a few days, and then on maybe to Southern Ireland, to lie low for as many months as he could before he needed to find a new post, a new identity.

He was as sure as he could be that he had not been followed and that no-one had been told where he was, and was almost beginning to feel at peace with himself after weeks of anxiety.

He pottered around the saloon area; making a sandwich with some ham and cheese, heating some tomato soup, making a large mug of cocoa.

McAdams sat eating and drinking and stared out of the cabin window at the night. Moonlight dappled the gently undulating ocean. There was a clear sky above him on this crisp, late Spring night. The stars stood out in a way they simply didn't in the light polluted city. He closed all the curtains on the boat, switched on the radio and enjoyed half an hour of Radio 3.

Tiredness suddenly overwhelmed him. Whether it was the lateness of the hour or the gently undulating rocking of the boat he did not know, but he was glad to make his way forward into the main cabin and climb into his sleeping bag. Within seconds he was asleep.

After an hour or so, McAdams was awake suddenly, he thought as a result of a full-formed idea that had popped into his dreams. He felt for the laptop he had by the bed, fired up the hard drive and punched in his password. The screen flared brightly. He had suddenly thought of the final paragraph for his paper and feverishly typed it in while he still remembered it.

He had only just saved the file and was closing the laptop when there was a bump and the boat suddenly lurched sideways. There was the sound of boots jumping onto the deck aft.

His heart in his mouth, McAdams pushed the laptop under the edge of cushion on the bunk next to him and struggled out of the sleeping bag. The dawn light greeted him as he pushed his way out of the cabin to meet the threat.

McAdams pushed through the cabin door just as the boarders entered the companionway and climbed down to the saloon. McAdams was carrying a spare steel stanchion he'd had ready. He waved it at the three intruders as they crowded into the galley area.

"Good morning, Dr McAdams." Cousins, dressed all in black, raised his palms in supplication. "Please don't be alarmed. My name is Cousins. From your employer, Howarth-Weaver. I've been sent to find you. People were worried about you. Your sister is worried about you. Can you put the weapon down. Please?"

McAdams looked at the two burly men behind the thin raven-like figure of Cousins. He noted with a sinking feeling in the pit of his stomach that all three men wore latex gloves.

"This is no social call, Mr Cousins." He tried to sound as menacing as he could. "Get off my boat. Now."

"I just wanted to talk, Dr McAdams, to hear your side of the story, to help you, if I can. Can I sit down? Maybe we can have a little drink. He drew a half-bottle of whisky from his pocket.

"I'm teetotal. And it's dawn, for God's sake. Why would anyone want a drink?"

But Cousins was undeterred and was smilingly gathering some glasses from the galley. "Let's sit down and be friends, eh?"

McAdams decided to take the initiative. While Cousins was sliding into the bench round the table McAdams raised the stanchion and whirled it leftwards at Cousins's head. The stanchion connected with Cousins's left cheek, and he was catapulted against the cabin wall. McAdams hurled himself forwards. Hoping to barge his way aft, up the companionway and out into the dawn air, where he would jump into the sea. He reasoned he was not too far from the shore and would rather risk a lengthy swim in the freezing water than fight it out onboard.

The hired men brought by Cousins were not as willowy as the company lawyer and merely planted themselves in front of the scientist as he tried his best to escape. It was as if they were two solid menhirs of stone. He had tried, but there was no escape.

Four heavily muscled arms gripped McAdams as tight as they could and sat him, with relentless force, down on the bench opposite Cousins. Cousins was still nursing his face. "Well," he said. "That'll be a nice bruise. Thank you so much, Doctor. You've decided that this isn't going to be easy, haven't you?"

"What do you want?" McAdams glared at Cousins.

"Well, for a start. Where are all the papers from your

project? And the copies? They belong to my clients. Whatever you did working on their dollar, belongs to them."

"You have my team's offices and labs. You have my team's filing cabinets, desks, PCs. You've got it all."

"But the copies?" asked Cousins. "Who has them? You? Or your two co-workers. Do you have notebooks, card files maybe? Do you have them?" McAdams shook his head.

"So it's all just in your head is it?" McAdams nodded thinking that maybe this might lead to some bargaining position. But Cousins did not follow this up. He appeared satisfied that whatever work he referred to existed solely in McAdams's head. "And your co-workers. They aren't on board. Anyone can see that. Where did they go, Doctor? Where are they? Where are Corrine Lloyd and Marcus Zuckerman?"

"How did you find me?" asked McAdams.

Cousins fixed his gaze on a briefcase sitting on the bench. He drew it over to himself. "Let's have a look shall we?" He pulled out odds and ends. Minutes of extinct committee meetings, a book by Cohen on Molecular Modelling, some half-chewed pencils, a half-consumed bottle of Diet Coke and at the bottom of the briefcase, a bleep. "Oh, the company bleep," smiled Cousins. "Led us straight to you."

"I switched it off," protested McAdams.

"It has GPS positioning on all the time. We just triangulated your position and hired a boat. Are you wondering whether your colleagues were stupid enough to keep their bleeps too?" Cousins laughed. "To allay your fears . . . Lloyd and Zuckerman . . . they were brighter than you. Now then, have I covered everything?" He mused silently over his conversation with McAdams. His cheek was hurting badly, and accordingly his concentration was not as sharp as he would have liked it. "Well, we found you, that's the main thing. I didn't think you would tell us where your colleagues were. Never mind. Let's move things on before people wake up onshore." He nodded to one of his men, "Go and check up top, see if it's clear." He looked at the other man and nodded. His second man reached for a small bottle in his pocket.

Cousins narrowed his soulless eyes. "Now, Dr McAdams. Are you going to make this a bit easier for yourself? Will you take a drink?" Cousins gestured to the half bottle of whisky and the glasses on the table. "And then take all these pills, please?" He removed a brown plastic bottle of amitriptyline tablets from his pocket.

McAdams tried one last time to escape, reasoning that one thug would be easier to get past than two. He made it to the bottom of the companionway, and the heavy weight of a fist slammed into his neck. He fell heavily cutting his head. Blood spurted. He stumbled up and was cuffed again to fall once more. Then he was dragged upwards, pushed back down into his seat.

"I guess you won't comply," said Cousins. They were the last words McAdams ever heard. A cloth soaked in ether was pressed to his face. He struggled to stay awake, but lost and slumped. Strong arms held him upright so Cousins could take the next phase forward.

Cousins looked at the unconscious scientist and withdrew

a rubbery coil of wide-bore tubing from his pocket. He covered the tip in jelly from a tube and pushed it expertly into one of McAdams's nostrils and fed it back through the nasal space and down his pharynx and into his oesophagus. After passing a good length of tubing he paused, attached a syringe and drew back. He was gratified to find about 110ml of stomach juices coming back. Reasoning he hadn't passed the tube into McAdams's trachea he discarded the syringe into a paper refuse bag along with the ether soaked cloth. He took a funnel and wedged it in the end of the tube and held it aloft. He poured the half bottle of whisky down the funnel. It gurgled down the nasogastric tube. And into the unconscious man's belly. Next Cousins tried to unscrew the tablet bottle. He struggled a bit with the child safety top, cursing and raising his eyebrows ironically at the thug who cradled McAdams's body. Triumphing over the resistant plastic Cousins emptied the tiny red 100mg pills down the funnel to cascade down the tube, rattling into his stomach. Four or five pills would have been enough to trigger abnormal cardiac rhythms. With the bottle empty, Cousins began tidying up after himself. "Keep him upright, we need the tablets to go down his gut."

Cousins went into the Stern cabin and was about to make a search when a shout came from the man above. "There's a fishing ship – it's about a mile away. Looks as if its heading this way."

"Damn," said Cousins. He knew that the fishermen might never notice the two boats clustered together as they were – Cousins's craft and McAdams's boat – or then again they might be interested in them and might remember them. "We've got to get going. Take him up. Put him over the side – away from them." He called up to the man on the deck. "Draw up the anchor on this boat." Cousins followed the others up the companionway. He looked back, checking that they had left no identifying traces. He carried McAdams's briefcase with him. There were smears of McAdams's blood, but there was no time to clean this up. The smears would only lead to McAdams. And would be a dead end.

Cousins heard the splash as McAdams's body hit the water. Then Cousins was clambering onto the craft they had all come in. They unhitched themselves from McAdams's boat, which was now left to drift, empty on the waves.

The fishermen on board the fishing boat were having coffee and bacon rolls from their own galley, and never noted the two boats separating. One headed off at speed; the other drifted silently eastwards. McAdams's unconscious body, devoid of breath and heartbeats, floated for a while.

SEVEN

Pamela, Lynch's wife, had concocted a form of vegetarian cuisine for Power. Power had enjoyed Aubergine Moussaka with a glass of chilled Chablis and then a simple fruit salad. She eyed him thoughtfully over the family dinner table, "These are big changes, Carl. Moving on from your job and becoming a vegetarian. What's prompted all this?"

Power wondered what Lynch had told Pamela. "Well, it's more about things changing around me rather than me changing," he said. "The hospital has changed so much. It's a business now, taking on huge mortgages from the Private Finance Initiative, and I don't seem to fit in anymore. The hospital wants its staff to be components. They seem to prefer expensive locums that can be ordered about and don't cause trouble. Like the one I met last week who's covering a colleague. The secretaries showed me his clinic letters – he always writes the same thing about patients – that they are well, have no concerns and have no suicidal plans. He never changes their medicines. His notes in their records are the same. He does this for about two weeks and moves on. If anything happens to the patient he just shrugs and says 'when I saw them they were well and had no suicidal ideas'. He's moved on by then – several thousand pounds richer. No responsibilities."

"But if there was a problem. If somebody needed help?" asked Lynch.

"He's gone before anybody notices," said Power. He's like a chameleon; he looks like a doctor, talks like a doctor, but does nothing. Camouflage. And he's exactly what the managers like. Like a cardboard cutout or a fake soldier propped up on the castle walls."

"What will you do?" asked Pamela.

"I don't know yet," said Power. "I'm thinking." He had been thinking for a while, but nothing had occurred to him.

"Well," said Pamela. "I hope you're not going to move down South or go abroad. That explains the leaving of the hospital, but the diet?"

"I'm not sure its safe to eat meat anymore," said Power. "I've had a few young patients with dementia, and as far as I can tell, it's prion disease . . . from meat. A new discovery. There've been several cases reported in *The Lancet.* And those few cases maybe the tip of the iceberg. I think it is safer to cut it out of my diet."

"I'm not sure I could do without meat," said Lynch. He particularly loved Lamb Hot Pot.

Pamela said nothing and began clearing the glasses away. She would like to see Power happy and settled down. Power was not aware of her plans for his domesticity as he collected plates, followed her to the kitchen, and placed them in the sink before rejoining Lynch.

"You're not selling your house as well are you?" asked Lynch.

He was a big admirer of Power's Victorian mansion, Alderley House.

"No, I don't think so," said Power. "Although the village has changed so much. Difficult to recognize it nowadays. Full of money from bankers and footballers and their wives in big sunglasses and shiny, black BMWs. You wish they'd all go away."

"Okay," said Lynch. "Don't make too many changes. I think Pamela is a bit worried about you."

They fell to talking about the McAdams case. Power related about his meeting with Sarah Ferguson.

"And Cousins stayed with them, almost keeping them hostage in their house over the period of the Inquest, like he was controlling them."

"Even to sitting outside their bedroom through the night, in darkness and silence," Lynch shuddered. "What kind of a solicitor does that? His role seems to be more than that of a solicitor to Howarth-Weaver. And the team that McAdams had at the company, why break it up? Why did they do this, and if they played a role in McAdams's death, what is the motive?"

"Maybe the other members of the team can tell us?"

"But where are they? What do they know? They've both gone to ground. Sent away by McAdams – to save their souls. But where to? And they are silent. We do need to talk; I agree." He frowned. "Maybe they are already dead? If Cousins was so keen to control the sister, Sarah, at the Inquest, so invested in the outcome, he would stop at nothing to find Corrine Lloyd and Marcus Zuckerman. It wouldn't make sense to stop at murdering Dr McAdams. He would need to silence them all. I'm surprised that Sarah Ferguson is still alive. I can understand why she is so frightened. And as for Cousins himself . . . he's like a ghost. I can't contact him. Their offices deny he even exists. He's vanished into the mist. "

"How's that possible?"

"These big corporations are multinational. They have their own security departments – industrial espionage is the norm. You have no idea, Carl. We will only see Cousins when he wants to be seen."

Power pushed the frail fragment of paper Sarah had given him across the table to his friend. "This is all we have to go on," said Power. "It seems McAdams gave this to his sister. To phone if anything happened to him. It's a mobile number. There's no answer though. Its meant to be Corrine Lloyd's phone."

"And this number. Could Cousins have it?"

"I don't think so. It was a dedicated phone given to Corrine by McAdams. McAdams asked his sister to guard it with her life until someone came who would listen to her."

"You, I guess," said Lynch. He made a note of the number and waved the transcript in Power's direction. "This is a huge advantage. If Cousins doesn't have the number, and we can use it to trace Corrine Lloyd's phone, we have the upper hand . . ."

* * *

Power put the phone down after hearing bad news from the neurologist about his patient, Adam. Power put his head in his hands and leant forward onto a big pile of clinic notes on his desk. He wondered if he had the strength to push on through an afternoon clinic. Looking up, he reached for the phone again and dialed Laura's number. He made an urgent plea for sweet black coffee. She sounded a little brusque, "Well, I will, but if you are really going then bear in mind that I won't be your handmaiden much longer!" Power's term of notice ran out in a few days. He would be gone from the hospital after just one more ward round and two clinics.

"I'm sorry," said Power. "I've had some bad news about Adam. He was on the ward recently; you typed his discharge letter."

"So?" She was clipped and clearly irritable. Power did not understand why.

"He's got advanced prion dementia. It's been confirmed."

"Oh," she said, finally understanding Power's distress. Her voice softened. "He's so young though."

"Yes," said Power. "It doesn't seem fair, really."

"I'll get you a coffee. You need it; I think." Power nodded although she couldn't see him. As he replaced the receiver, the phone rang again.

It was Lynch.

"Carl, have you had any luck with the laptop?"

"No," said Power. "I've tried nearly all the passwords I can think of. I think of new ideas, the more I learn of McAdams."

"Keep on trying. I've had more luck with the phone

though." At this point, Laura came through the door bearing hot, sweet coffee. She placed it in front of him on the desk and, not wishing to interrupt, for the first time ever put a hand on his shoulder. She gave his shoulder a squeeze and briefly their eyes met. Something different seemed to be in her look as she made her way out of his office. Power was puzzled and struggled to focus on the phone conversation. "Are you there, Carl?" Lynch was asking.

"Yes, sorry." Power raised the steaming coffee to his lips. The mug smelled of Laura somehow, and he began to think how he would miss her. "You were saying about the phone. Did you try it? Did she answer?"

"No," said Lynch. "She's not answering. She's out of this country and I think I know where."

"How do you know?"

"I have my contacts," Lynch laughed. "Don't tell anybody, please, but if you can make the right case to a contact of mine at GCHQ, they will help trace a mobile using technology on loan from their American cousins. This is a technology that Cousins won't have at his disposal. Or at least I don't think so."

"Well, he doesn't have the number in any case," said Power.

"Even more reason to think that we are ahead of him then," said Lynch.

"Where is she?"

"Not on this line, Carl, it won't be secure. I will meet you for a drink later. The only difficulty is that if she is abroad I don't have the resources to send someone overseas to question her. It would take finance and human resources that just aren't in our budget."

"That's all right," Power found himself saying, to his own surprise. "I'm not doing anything next week. I'll go."

* * *

Power had already endured a seven-hour flight from Manchester to Philadelphia and he was now broiling in the humid heat of Philadelphia airport and scurrying through crowds of people, he was panicking that he would miss his connection and felt burdened by his heavy luggage. He was fussed, flustered and sweaty and irritated to near screaming pitch by the teeming masses of people in front who seemed determined to frustrate his chance of ever reaching the security check in time. He had not been out of the airport building, but he hated Philadelphia with an irrational passion. He had planned to get something to eat and to relax after the first leg of his journey, but there was no time after struggling through US border control and collecting his luggage.

The heroism of his valiant struggle through one side of the airport to the other to get to the flight on time was not recognized by the check-in agents for his flight to Raleigh in North Carolina, who glared at him with undisguised animosity and snarled, "You're the last one."

"I'm sorry," he almost stammered. His mouth felt dry, and the words came out wrong. "The customs . . . the passport people . . ."

His luggage was grabbed from him and stuffed on a conveyor belt to the underworld of the airport. Disapproving glances and silent nods of the head directed him to the still open double doors that led down to American Airlines Flight 4588 to Raleigh Airport. As he hurried down the corridor the doors were closed behind him and as he entered the plane the other passengers, all seated and waiting to depart, stared at him as he was shown to his lonely seat at the rear of the plane. He tried to look ahead of him and avoid the stares he was getting.

He sank into the seat and closed his eyes to block everything out. The neighbouring passenger was somewhat overlarge, and a warm apron of fat spilled over the seat arm and intruded onto Power. Power felt mildly nauseated as he tried to meditate and block out the outside world.

Two hours later at Terminal 2 of Raleigh Airport his suitcase failed to materialize. Power stood forlornly by the carousel long after all the other passengers had departed. He watched the slats of black rubber going round and round and realised that although he could stand there as long as he liked his suitcase would not appear. He gripped his shoulder bag and reassured himself that he still had McAdams's laptop.

After reporting his lost luggage, he hired a car and drove to the Hampton Hotel on Capital Boulevard. He drank complimentary iced tea as the receptionist drilled him through his check-in, and finally he stumbled into the lift, along the orange-carpeted corridors and into his room. He put a 'do not disturb' sign on the door handle outside, closed the door resolutely and flopped face down on the bed, groaning. Within seconds, he was asleep.

Power woke, sticky with the heat and dry mouthed. He had slept solidly for fourteen hours, but with the time difference was still early for breakfast. He showered and put on a short-sleeved white shirt, blue shorts and sandals and wandered down to the lobby. He gulped three glasses of orange juice and several mugs of coffee as he munched through waffles and bowls of fruit salad.

Restored, he made his way out to his hire car in the car park. As he left the dark, air-conditioned lobby, the morning sunlight blazed around him, bleaching his vision into nothingness. A wave of superheated air wafted around him when he opened the door. He struggled to get into the car and switched the engine on as soon as he could, willing the air-conditioning to provide an instant miracle of cold air. The miracle was not forthcoming, and there was no instantaneous relief from the gasp-inducing heat. Power stuck to the car seat uncomfortably as the air-conditioning flickered into life and feebly provided him with lukewarm air. Power consulted a map, trying to find the University of North Carolina that Lynch had identified as the source of the mobile signal.

He drove down the wide baking streets, past green oceans of evergreen trees, to the University district.

* * *

The tiny cream-coloured *Anopheles* larvae wriggled and

writhed in the still water captured within the mountains of used tyres behind the compound fences. Their bulbous heads waved through the water as they prepared to pupate. Two days later they would become adults. The compound near the Pista Suburbana road in Managua had thousands of used tyres – some prestige ones stacked up in columns or mid-range tyres in mountainous heaps. On the other side of the compound's perimeter fence was a playing field, which stood in front of the American School of Nicaragua. The school year had finished, and the children had gone, but this year it was hosting a Summer Conference – with five hundred high school delegates participating in mock UN debates. A camp of two hundred tents stood on the school playing fields. Adult female mosquitoes from the compound – graduates of the schools of larvae in the water-filled tyres flew over the tents at dawn and dusk.

They were a new generation of the mosquitoes planted there by one of Cousins's team from Howarth-Weaver.

In their tents the children had breathed out carbon dioxide and accordingly the mosquitoes had headed for this stream of billowing gas, indicating the crowd of respiring living animals, and those children in the camp which the females deemed had just the right human body odours to home in on. In the mosquitoes' bellies were the newly bred strains of *Plasmodium falciparum*. And as the mosquitoes alighted on the children's skin they nuzzled their way about the skin with their needle-like probosces looking for blood vessels for the necessary blood meal to make their eggs. In the search for the blood meal the mosquitoes would transfer the malarial parasite, the *Plasmodium* sporozoite which would make its way via the blood stream to the children's livers to produce tens of thousands of new life forms over the next two weeks or so.

At lunchtime, the young delegates laughed and chatted over a meal of rice and beans (gallo pinto) and fried plantains (platanos frito). Some drank granadilla and some drank fizzy water. Some of them nursed a series of red bites from the mosquitoes. Symptoms would start as early as a week later.

Having fed during the day, the females would make their way over to the still waters in the tyres in the compound and tonight, as the infected children from the conference lay asleep in their tents, the female mosquitoes would lay small rafts of their eggs in the water.

That night, each species, mosquito and human, would be wholly unaware of the transfer of the parasites between them earlier in the day.

* * *

The University of North Carolina campus was flat and broad, with trimmed green lawns punctuated by paths of white concrete that glared steamily under the relentless sun. Power trudged along the wide paths of the campus towards the Department of Molecular Biomedical Sciences. He looked at the gaggle of young students that wandered past him, some drinking coffee and others slooshing down water from plastic bottles. The sight made him thirsty. Power found the Department in a range of smart, brick-built neo-Georgian buildings.

Inside the air-conditioned lobby was a water fountain from which Power drank thirstily. He splashed some drops of water onto his perspiring face. The secretary watched amusedly from the reception window. Power straightened up and felt his shirt sticking to his back. In the air-conditioned lobby he began to feel somewhat cool.

"Hello," he said to the secretary. "Can you help me, please?" And he gave her winning smile.

" I can try, sure." She smiled back at the handsome, young doctor.

"My name is Dr Power, Dr Carl Power." He proffered his Hospital ID card. "I can give you telephone contacts you can ring to verify my identity." He was thinking of giving her Lynch's number at the Cheshire Constabulary.

"How can I help you, Dr Power?"

"I'm hoping to speak to a researcher here, Dr Corrine Amy Lloyd. I've come from England to talk to her, please could you ask her?"

"I'm sorry, but there's no Dr Lloyd here." At these words, she saw Dr Power's face fall.

"Nobody joined the Faculty from England recently? Last few weeks?"

"I shouldn't really say, Dr Power, but we do have a researcher Corrine who arrived from England a month or so back. I can speak to her for you?" She was rewarded by a grin from Power as she picked up the phone and punched in an extension number. She introduced Dr Power and handed the phone over to him.

"Hello? This is Dr Power."

"Er . . . hello? I don't think I know you. Who are you?"

"No, we haven't met. I am . . . a doctor . . . a consultant from England. I was sent here by Sarah, Sarah Ferguson. Fergus's sister." Power imagined Corrine mulling things over maybe a few doors away or maybe far away else in another part of the University altogether. "I'm hoping to speak to Corrine Amy Lloyd."

"I am Dr Corrine Williams. I'm not sure I can help you."

"If you were Dr Lloyd you could help me a great deal. And I think I could help you. I am genuine. Corrine, you can phone the police in the UK, if you like. Ask for the number of Cheshire Constabulary in England. You can phone them and ask to speak to Superintendent Lynch. He will vouch for me. They will even fax you my photo so you can verify who I am."

"Are you the man who listens?"

"Sarah said something like that. She thinks I am. She said that Fergus had told her to wait for the man who listened, not the one who asked."

"I might meet you in public somewhere, Dr Power. Let me write down the name of the police officer you mentioned."

"Superintendent Lynch."

There was a pause as she committed the name to paper. She spoke softly, "If I decide to meet you, Dr Power, I will phone you tomorrow morning at your hotel to tell you where and when. I need to think about things. If I don't phone by twelve noon, please don't ever try to contact me again, just leave me alone. What is your hotel called?"

"The Hampton Hotel on Capital Boulevard."

"All right, Dr Power. But I'm not promising anything. Now, please can you leave the University? I'm sorry to be inhospitable. I hope you understand. Please go now and wait at your hotel."

* * *

So anxious was he not to miss any phone call that Power alerted the hotel reception desk that he was expecting an important call and arranged for a breakfast in his room. He munched his way through doughnuts, fruit salad and glugged down what seemed to be a bucket full of black coffee. He then watched TV – a double dose of Maury programmes – where a silver-haired journalist babbled about psychotherapy while conjuring with DNA paternity tests, revealing the magical results like some priest divining sacrificial entrails.

At eleven thirty Power's mobile phone buzzed once. A text from Lynch, "Was asked to speak to Dr. Corrine Amy Lloyd by Control Desk. Confirmed your identity. Everything okay? Lynch."

As Power was texting back about his anxieties about the impending deadline of noon and the lack of a phone call from Corrine, the hotel phone rang from the bedside table and he scrambled over the bed to reach it.

"Hello? Carl Power here?"

"It's Corrine. I spoke to your Superintendent. He vouched for you. I will meet you in the foyer of the North Carolina Museum of History at two p.m. today. It's on Edenton Street."

Power had only just scribbled the name down when she rang off.

He was so anxious to meet that he gathered his things immediately and made his way downstairs. The twenty-minute taxi journey meant he was there over an hour early. For want of anything better to do he wandered through the free exhibits, documenting the State history of North Carolina. He emerged from the exhibits some half an hour later somewhat bemused by an account of the State's Confederate position during the civil war, its dependence on the death-implicated industry of tobacco, and its embracement of slavery. He shivered at a wall of twenty Klu Klux Klan masks that was both terrifying to behold and offered without any insightful comment. The absence of comment led Power to conclude that the movement in North Carolina was still not to be offended.

It was a bemused Dr Power that emerged into a twee gift shop that seemed removed from the horrors of history he had observed. He felt hungry again, but there was no café to anaesthetize his disquiet with food. He felt unable to pass the gift shop counter without asking a question, "Can I ask about the museum? Is the museum meant to promote the State, or is it meant to deter anybody from settling here?"

The gift shop lady looked at him through owlish glasses,

and smiled the complacent smile of the insightless, "Why – it's a celebration of our journey!"

"I see," said Dr Power and meandered into the foyer.

He sat down by a water fountain and mused on the perplexing exhibits. He was so preoccupied that he almost didn't notice a small bird-like woman in a sparrow-brown twin set, alighting on the bench beside him. She pulled out a packet of ham sandwiches and proffered one to Dr Power. "A sandwich, Dr Power?"

"No thanks," he looked hungrily at the sandwich. "I don't eat meat anymore."

"Oh," she said, and replaced the food in her handbag. "There's a bar over the road. They might have some food for you."

Power nodded. "It would be good to leave this place." Coming out of his preoccupied state Power realised that this sharp-eyed young woman was the person he had flown nearly four thousand miles to see. "You must be Dr Lloyd?"

She nodded, watching him inquisitively. "Have you been around the history exhibits?"

"It was just a neutral place I chose for us to meet in. I've never been inside."

Power suggested they adjourn to the bar she had mentioned and they left the museum with Power suppressing a shudder as they walked into the North Carolina sun.

The bar was showing a baseball game and a cluster of staff and patrons were gathered around a big screen. They ordered a beer, which Power found watery, and Dr Lloyd asked for a red wine. He scanned the menu for anything vaguely vegetarian.

"The US is not really a vegetarian-friendly place," observed Power to his companion and in his head chose blueberry pancakes.

"People's diets here are dictated by big companies who want to sell saturated fat, cream, milk, beef and corn syrup," said Dr Lloyd. "The industry sells what it wants to the people and lives off them like a parasite living off its host. Only the industry here is killing the host with obesity and diabetes."

Put off his first option of pancakes from the menu, Power opted for a Tuna Nicoise. His guest sipped her glass of Cellar 8 Cabernet.

"How are you coping out here?" asked Power.

"It's been a big change. One minute you are working on a successful research project. You've developed a drug that is safe to take, that does its job. Do you know how many drug molecules we try out that fail? How difficult it is to get to a place where you've synthesized something that is stable, that doesn't kill people, or doesn't cause horrendous side effects, and that actually does what you intended, and does it well? Something that saves lives. You wait a lifetime – a whole career to get that. Thousands of researchers never get that far." She sounded angry. "And then, overnight, you are whisked away from all that . . . and it's gone." She took another sip. "Don't misunderstand me, Dr Power. I'm not ungrateful to Fergus . . . for arranging my exit, my escape. It's just that I hadn't realised what a wrench it would be. How different things would be."

"I was at his Inquest," said Power. "I was asked to look into the possibility of suicide."

She looked away, and her eyes briefly filled with tears. "He saved me, but he couldn't save himself. And did you think it was suicide, Dr Power?" Power shook his head. "No, it was no suicide," she said. "I know that. Because he knew what was coming. When they shut the programme down. When they moved us to another division and we lost access to our labs and our mainframe computer. He knew we had just a few days. He wasted time on me and on Marcus Zuckerman . . . arranging our departure before his own. I don't know how he did it, but he arranged a flight out to Europe, then a name change, another flight into Africa, a new name again and finally this identity here in this State – where they accept me – where one of his old colleagues was able to get a job for me – for someone with a made up CV, just on trust. And it's here I must re-build my tattered career – make a new name for myself and start again writing academic papers in someone else's name. When I should be winning prizes in my own name, for a decade's work on Plasmosid." Her hands trembled with frustration and the meniscus of the wine in the glass between her fingers shook.

"Tell me about Plasmosid, what was so special about this?"

"What do you know about malaria, Dr Power?"

"Oh, it's a while since I studied this. My knowledge is basic – it's a tropical infectious disease caused by small parasites – *Plasmodium vivax* or *Plasmodium falciparum* I seem to recall – passed on to humans by mosquitoes when they feed. It can affect the brain, the liver, the blood stream, it causes high fevers every few days. You treat it with quinine or similar drugs."

"You are right, up to a point, Dr Power, but a bit out of date. You know it was a killer that laid armies low, stopped Empires expanding in their tracks. It's killed millions over the years and outbreaks have been recorded in nineteenth century London, and as far north as Sweden, Finland and Russia where there was an outbreak in the nineteen-twenties. When the English white settlers tried to move into malaria areas in Africa, they succumbed in droves. They had a rhyme: 'Beware beware, the Bight of Benin: one goes out where fifty went in'. Malaria's been with us for centuries, probably millennia. Chaucer described a tertian fever – an ague – in the Canterbury Tales, which can only have been malaria contracted in England in the fourteenth century. It always was a global infection, and now we have new strains of *Plasmodium* that are resistant to quinolones. Our drugs have stopped working. And the insecticides we used to kill the mosquitoes that pass the *Plasmodium* on are either no longer effective or too toxic to use. There will be a pandemic of treatment –resistant malaria if we are not careful. With thousands of deaths worldwide. And that is why Plasmosid was so important."

"You said 'was', but surely . . ."

"When I said we were turned out of our labs and we had no access to the mainframe, I meant you to understand that I have no records, Dr Power. None of my data is available to me. I couldn't synthesise the molecule without my schematics, and the detailed convergent synthesis process is finely tuned and sequenced – I don't have access to the sequences I designed. They are far too complex to just commit to memory. If I had my notes or the paper Fergus was working on, I could synthesise the molecule within weeks. Without that paper, it would take me, even with what I remember, maybe a year."

"So you were a team . . . that depended on each other . . . needed each other to work?"

"Absolutely, we were a very small team in actual fact . . . For what we were trying to do. But Howarth-Weaver seemed to like small teams. They could control things that way as it has turned out." She finished her wine and Power signaled to the bartender for more wine, but decided against another thin beer and ordered another glass of red. "We could access other advice from the company – like statistics – but Fergus was our leader, I was in charge of the organic chemistry, and Zuckerman was the medic, who co-ordinated the field trials."

"And the field trials were successful?"

"Absolutely," said Lloyd. "We trialled it over two years in several places and ways – there was an open trial with nearly two thousand patients with multi-drug resistant malaria in Thailand. A 99% recovery rate with Plasmosid alone. Some 20% or so got side effects of things like dizziness, sleep problems, nausea, and loss of appetite, but no great drop-out rates. It was a success. A gold plated 100% success."

"So why not roll it out with fanfares?"

She shrugged and pointed to a group of fat office workers guzzling beer and munching on pretzels and fries as they watched TV. "Why not only sell people reasonably sized, nutritious portions of healthy fish and fruit and vegetables? Why sell tobacco and alcohol when you know they kill people?"

"I don't understand," said Power.

"It's kind of endearing that you don't understand," said Lloyd, eyeing him, her head on one side. "But the answer is in a financial equation, Dr Power. And you and I probably don't fit into that equation. Plasmosid doesn't make the most profit and so it isn't needed. And so we all need to be eliminated so the equation can balance again."

"And that's what Howarth-Weaver is like?"

"It's like the world Dr Power, a mixed-up place, but as far as I can see, from my perspective, Howarth-Weaver is a very dark, mixed-up place."

"Is there no light there?"

"It's a family firm, did you know that? Despite its size, it is still run by one family. One generation. Three siblings. Two brothers. One sister. There's bad blood between them I think. The first born, the sister, was trained up by daddy as the head. She's a bit of an idealist I think, but I'm not sure. I think they're probably all a lost cause."

"But she might be able to get access to the files you need."

Corrine snorted and took a long swig of wine. "Howarth-Weaver are nothing if not thorough. If they'd taken the decision to eliminate an idea and were so committed that they'd kill to do so, do you really think that they'd leave some papers lying around? Or leave our computer systems available for interrogation? They were destroyed. Fergus was very clear about their intent. And he was right about their determination wasn't he? He put his life on the line, and they took it."

"Did Fergus entrust you with any password?" asked Power.

"No. He did not, Dr Power. He gave me nothing."

"Would the third member of the team have any information? A paper that McAdams was writing? Or a password?"

"You mean Dr Zuckerman? I don't know. I doubt it. Fergus thought he was protecting us by not giving us the information, so I doubt he'd give Zuckerman anything either."

Power paused. The crowd around the screen watching the baseball match was roaring in approval. He waited till their noise died down. "I'd like to speak with Dr Zuckerman, please – to see if he can give me any clues. If you know where he is?"

"I think I should phone him, maybe, first. To see if he minds. I suppose it wouldn't hurt to let you know that Fergus found him a research post in Peru."

"Peru!"

"Deepest, darkest Peru, in a city you can only reach by plane or boat. There, I've said too much. I will phone him and then let you know if he's willing to speak. Oh, I never checked . . . this is all confidential?"

"Of course," said Power.

"I just kind of started talking without checking that out. I guess you just have that way about you."

"I won't be letting you down," said Power.

"What are you going to do?"

"I still don't know for sure why the company would want to destroy all trace of a successful drug . . . a drug that would save lives. What would lead to them killing the main researcher . . . and what to stop it all? Maybe this elder sister is the key. Maybe she could stop it all? And maybe – is there nothing we can do to save the drug research?"

"I'm not sure what can be done. You're just one person against a vast company. If they don't want you to succeed . . . well, you won't. You could give up now, and save yourself a lot of bother." She said this, but she had already summed Dr Power up as a man who did not give up. "Although I was reading a briefing earlier from the United Nations monitoring service and they are picking up a spike in malaria cases. The same treatment-resistant strain. In five different countries." Power looked into her piercing eyes. "That doesn't happen in nature, Dr Power. That's the hand of man at work."

"What can be done, without the drug . . . what did you call it?"

"Plasmosid is what Fergus named it. And what can be done? We go back to the old methods. Try some combinations of old drugs, I suppose, but they will likely fail against this new resistant strain. There will be thousands of cases. And remember that the current human global population is less resistant. The mortality rate will be somewhere shy of 20%. So it's back to the old methods – war on the mosquito that carries the *Plasmodium* – good drainage systems to avoid collections of stagnant water, putting oil on the surface of the water, spraying walls with insecticides every few months, sleeping under insecticide soaked nets, screens on windows. There's also a bacillus that can be used to kill the mosquito larvae being trialled. But every infected human is just a walking reservoir for the disease, and the mosquitoes just pass it on. It will take a great battle Dr Power, fought on many fronts and the drug would have been key."

Power looked at her. "Is there anything else you think I should know?"

She shook her head. "You can come back and ask me if you want to know anymore." He nodded, but a sense of foreboding made him wonder if there would be such an opportunity.

"Will you let me know what Dr Zuckerman says please? I'd like to see him." He wrote his mobile number on a name card from his pocket. "His account might add something – complement your view."

"Oh, Dr Zuckerman and I didn't really get on, Dr Power, it was Fergus who lead and balanced the team, but now Zuckerman and I – we are both exiles. And one day I'd like to get back to my mother, Dr Power. She's old now, and every day I wonder about her. I wonder is it safe to go home yet. I told her I'd be gone for a while, but when will it be safe? Will it ever be safe?"

"I don't know," said Power. He gave her another card. "These are the details of my friend, Superintendent Lynch. You've already spoken to him when you checked me out. If you have any worries. Need any help. He said you were to call him."

She nodded and put the cards away in her handbag. With one last look at Power, she nodded once and left without saying another word.

Power drained his glass of wine and stumbled outside into the heat to try and find a taxi to the hotel.

It was two p.m. in England when Power phoned Lynch. Lynch was sitting in his office at the computer reviewing his presentation for a lecture he would give at the Bruche Police Training School in Warrington that evening.

He was putting in details of the creation of the Cheshire Constabulary after a special Act of Parliament in 1829, when the phone rang.

He answered, "Superintendent Lynch."

"It's Carl, ringing from sticky Raleigh."

"Hot?"

"Humid."

"Did Dr Lloyd meet you eventually?"

"I've just got back from seeing her. She told me about the drug they were working on, Plasmosid. It was a success, but the company wasn't interested and closed them down. Destroyed their work. And we know what happened to McAdams . . . she was the one who designed the molecule and synthesized it. But it would take her a year or more to re-discover it without the data, which the company destroyed. Her life work gone."

"She still has her life. What's she doing now?"

"Trying to re-create her career. Under a new name. And re-invent herself in exile. Away from family and friends. On the quiet McAdams arranged a job for her in the biomedical faculty at the University through an old colleague."

"I see. So, what's to be done next?"

"I don't know. When pressed Dr Lloyd didn't know any password. Hadn't been given anything to hold on to by McAdams."

"Do you believe her – that she doesn't know anything?"

"Yes, I do. But we have two leads. One might be to approach the final scientist of the team – Zuckerman, and see if he has anything to help us. The second is to go to the top of the company in the hope that the left hand doesn't know what the right hand is doing."

"That would be a gamble."

"The Chief Executive is the eldest sister of the family, schooled by Dad since she was knee high to take over the firm. The strong, ethical one, I have been given to hope."

"You think she might be horrified to learn what has been going on in the company name? That she might intervene?"

"Yes. Lloyd implied there was some sort of split between the brothers and the sister. I know nothing more than that."

"Let me see if we have any information on her first, Carl. I'll do some digging about the background." Lynch started compiling a to-do list as he chatted. "And the other lead, Zuckerman, he might be the first to approach, where is he?"

"In deepest, darkest Peru, rather well hidden apparently in a city without a road in or out. That you can only travel to by plane or boat. That's all she would say. She promised to speak to him and let me know if he'd welcome a visit from me."

"What job would he be doing in Peru, to support himself? If McAdams arranged support at a University for Lloyd, what strings did he pull for Zuckerman. What was Zuckerman's role in the team?"

"A doctor – a researcher in tropical medicine probably – he ran the field trials for Plasmosid."

"Then Zuckerman will be doing a similar job in tropical medicine in Peru. Do you have any contacts you can ask about where that might be?"

"I'm not sure, let me think."

"I'll get out the geography books and see if I can find a city to match the details you gave. And Carl?"

"Yes?"

"Be careful. If we can work out where Zuckerman got a job, then others could eventually do the same."

* * *

Power put the phone down. He felt unable to leave the puzzle of where Zuckerman was alone. He felt he should not rely on Dr Lloyd or Lynch for some reason. There was no internet access in his room and so he wandered downstairs into the garishly, tartan-themed hotel lobby. He'd noticed a single computer available to guests for Internet access. He sat down at the computer amidst a sea of empty soft drink cans and noticed the screen was besmeared with jam. Crumbs littered the keyboard. He upended the keyboard and he shook most of the crumbs into the bin. The computer had been used to access gaming programs and the data hungry programs had filled the memory to capacity – the PC required a re-boot, which Power did.

He fired up the Netscape browser and opened the Altavista search engine and typed in 'Liverpool School of Tropical Medicine' to get their home page and scoured it for the UK phone number.

Having found it, he realised he probably had the phone number on the email of his Medical School colleagues that he'd received a few weeks before. Nevertheless, he was here now with the number in front of him. He drew out his mobile, punched in the International prefix and dialled the School's number.

A male voice. "Liverpool School of Tropical Medicine. Can I help you, please?"

"Is Dr Ross there please?"

"Putting you through, please hold."

"Hello?"

"Hello? This is Carl Power. We were at medical school together. This is Dr Ross?"

"Yes, it is. How are you, Carl?"

"I'm fine, what are you doing these days?"

"I'm a senior lecturer here. Plenty of trips abroad – Ghana, Sierra Leone, South East Asia. Never the nice bits though; it's strange how it's mainly the poor who live in the areas where there are epidemics. Are you still messing about in psychiatry?"

"Yes, still messing about. Can I ask you a serious question?

If you were a malaria specialist looking for a job in Peru, where would you work?"

"That's an odd question, for a psychiatrist."

"Indulge me, it's important. I'm trying to trace someone."

"Is it another of your women, Carl?" He could hear Ross smirking.

"No, it's serious. Life and death stuff, you know."

"Not psychiatry then," said Ross.

Power suppressed an urge to argue and sought to focus Ross. "Can you think of anywhere someone would work?"

"There's only here that's worth anything, Carl. This was the very first tropical medicine school. But there are loads of Universities in Peru, and there's a naval research unit in Lima – they look at diseases like malaria, dengue fever, yellow fever and the like. It might sound odd that the military are interested in disease, but in the past soldiers on shore and sailors on ships have been more devastated by tropical illness than fighting."

"Oh," said Power, thinking that none of these ideas for places seemed to fit. "Anywhere kind of remote, without roads going there?"

"Ah," said Ross. "You mean Iquitos. It's a city in the rainforest. You can get there by plane, or by river. It's a big city. Founded by the owners of rubber plantations. The naval research unit has an outpost there."

"Iquitos?"

"That's it. Can you tell me why you want to know?"

"I'm very grateful to you, but I can't say. I will take you out for a beer when I get back to England to say thanks. And maybe then I can tell you what I'm trying to do."

"Throw in a curry with that beer and you have a deal, Carl."

* * *

By the time he got back to the room he had received a text from Lynch.

Rather than getting on with his presentation on the history of the Cheshire Constabulary he had been thinking over what Power had said and been doing his own researches.

The text said: "Geographical clue points to city in forest – Iquitos. Have also considered your suggestion about interviewing CEO. Agree it is way forward, but keep me closely informed. Have DS Beresford finding her phone number for you. Her HQ in Toronto. Will send it next ten minutes. Lynch."

Power was reassured that two different methods of inquiry had led to the same solution, the rainforest city of Iquitos. He mused on how far he had journeyed and how far he had yet to go.

* * *

Power lay back on the pillows and considered what he could say to the Chief Executive of a multinational company. Reasoning that such a person was probably no different to anybody else and that Marianne Howarth-Weaver would have the same virtues and flaws, wants and desires as anybody else, he plucked up the courage to ring the number in Toronto that Lynch had texted him, using the hotel phone.

His phone call was answered within two rings. "Miss Howarth-Weaver's office," came the clipped efficient voice of her secretary.

"Good afternoon," said Dr Carl Power. "This is Dr Carl Power. Please can I speak to Marianne Howarth-Weaver."

"I'm sorry, Ms Howarth-Weaver does not take unsolicited calls. I am Gillian, her Personal Assistant. How can I help you?"

"Oh dear, I am sorry, but I do need to speak to Ms Howarth-Weaver herself. It is a very sensitive matter. It is about the company, about the malaria crisis and how the company should be helping more. It's sensitive because I need to make her aware of a problem inside the company, something which I hope she is unaware of."

"I'm sorry, Dr Power, what do you mean, that you hope she is unaware of? Ms Howarth-Weaver is fully briefed of all aspects of the company."

"I say that I hope she does not know about these aspects. I would hope that she is unaware, because I wouldn't like to think she is culpable, and I hope that once she is made aware that she will be minded to rectify what has gone wrong. I am hoping that my faith in her is not misplaced."

"Can I ask whether you are a journalist?"

"I am not."

"Are you wanting some kind of reward for this . . . information?"

"I am not. This is not a blackmail situation, nor am I

seeking to embarrass anyone. I am hoping that I can genuinely help your Chief Executive. I think once she hears what I have to say, she will want to take action. At least I can only pray she does."

There was a pause. She thought that there was undoubtedly a sincerity in Power's voice that was unusual in her day-to-day corporate life. "I will speak to Ms Howarth-Weaver. May I have a telephone number please, Dr Power?" He gave her the hotel's number.

Power lay back on the hotel bed watching a channel which seemed inexplicably to be replaying a variety program from the nineteen-sixties, with an orchestra composed of men in blue nylon suits with large lapels, with heads of long hair and immense, curly sideboards. He swigged a can of imported English beer and sighed with pleasure at the familiarity.

Twenty minutes later, Gillian rang. "Dr Power? This is Gillian. I'm pleased to say that Ms Howarth-Weaver has listened to what you said and does want to speak to you. But she doesn't want to speak to you on the phone. She wants to meet you face to face. I gather you are in the States? She has told me that the company will refund your travel to and from Toronto. She wants to invite you to her home on the Islands. Can you come here next week? Monday?"

"Yes," said Power. "Thank you for arranging this." He felt elated for the first time in weeks; hopeful at last.

"It's a pleasure, Dr Power. When you have details of your flight and time of arrival at Toronto airport, let me know and we will arrange your transport from there on in."

"Thank you so much," said Power.

Gillian said goodbye and put the phone receiver down for a moment. She picked it up again and punched in a familiar mobile number. It rang for a while as various phone servers located the mobile in whatever country it was then. Eventually, there was a click and a male answered.

"Cousins."

"Gillian here."

"Good afternoon, Gillian. What have you got for me?"

"Ms Howarth-Weaver has had a phone call from Dr Power."

Cousins sighed. "Yes, I met him in England. I thought he might be trouble. Did Marianne speak with him?"

"No, but she has asked to meet him next week. Do you want me to let the meeting go ahead?"

"Yes, I will need to take instructions on this myself, but unless you hear differently let it go ahead – I want to know exactly when and where though. Did he give you a phone number?"

"It was a hotel number."

"Yes, I'm looking your phone log now. It's a hotel in Raleigh, North Carolina. The Hampton chain. Thank you Gillian. Very helpful." The line went dead.

* * *

Power checked out of the Hampton Inn in Raleigh on a Sunday with feelings of gratitude that he would not visit the hotel again. He drove the baking hot car on a final journey to the rental zone at the airport. On the way he passed what looked like a school or a church, with a vast car park in front of it, full of cars. Glancing right, he assumed he was seeing a car boot sale, then noticed that the people milling about the car park were carrying armfuls of rifles and other guns. Open car boots contained an array of shotguns and ammunition and a sign boasted 'Raleigh Gun Show'. Power shook his head.

He unloaded the car, handed the keys over and wheeled his case and rucksack over to the airport bus.

He checked into his flight to Miami and passed relatively swiftly through security.

The automatic doors of the departure area swished behind him just as a thin, dark suited figure walked from the arrival gates into the main concourse of Raleigh Airport. He carried a single small case.

As Power had left North Carolina, Cousins had flown in.

EIGHT

Power stayed overnight at the Airport Sheraton in Miami. The air was drier than Raleigh, which he appreciated. He swam twenty lengths of the pool to wind down after the flight, dined on the patio on Cajun Sea Bass and Key West Shrimp and then fighting off a string of yawns fell into his bed.

Power slept solidly till three a.m.

In his dreamscape he was suddenly falling through clouds. The air was cold, and the sky whistled past him. Ice crystals from the clouds abraded his skin and spattered his face like needles. His arms and legs flailed uselessly in the air.

The clouds parted in front of him, and he could see a patchwork of fields and hedges and the diagonal sandstone escarpment of The Edge. He strained his eyes and could make out the roof of his home, Alderley House.

Somehow his fall had shrunk him to a point that he was lighter than air, and his precipitate plunge to earth became a leisurely drift groundwards. And yet the sense of threat did not leave Power's dream, for birds dived near him, swift harbingers of death for whom Power, reduced in size, was just a beakful of food.

All at once, he was down amongst the shoots of grass on his own lawn. The safety of the open front door of his house was visible across an expanse of gravel that was his drive.

Power was gearing himself up for a sprint to safety when a shadow fell over him. He looked up and in terror, saw a vast black raven. The raven eyed him, and its black beak loomed closer, opening. Power saw the raven's head turning into the face of Tuke, his past attacker. The curved mouthbeak opened to eat him.

He awoke cold and snarking for air. The air-conditioning was whirring and working overtime. Cold air blew into his face, which even so was slick with the sweat of fear. He struggled to find the light in the unfamiliar room and awoke panicked and breathless. He staggered over to the room thermostat and switched the air conditioning off. Its fan hummed to a halt. Power opened the windows to let the warmth of the Miami night into his room, to dispel the chill. Through the open window he heard the chirruping song of male cicadas calling out for mates and, reassured by the noise, sank back onto the dry side of the bed – opposite the place he had slept before. Shivering and troubled by intrusive images of his fight with Tuke on the cliff edge, Power drew the blankets round him and, shivering, waited for the Florida dawn over the golf course behind the hotel.

In the morning, he was irritable with the waitress over breakfast and irritable with the receptionist as he checked out, quibbling over items on his bill. He reflected on his sharp temper as he climbed into a taxi to go back to the airport. Since when had he become such a grump, he wondered? He initially blamed his disgruntlement on his poor night's sleep, but he knew the real answer. Irritability was a particular feature of

Post Traumatic Stress Disorder that could lead the sufferer into dangerous and uncharacteristic conflict. Power tried to suppress his ruminations on the possibility of his own illness, and his own potential need for treatment, but the nagging doubt that his resignation might just have been ill-considered and rooted in illness rather than motivated by any logical reason began to assail him.

Pushing the darkness of the night away, he focussed on the bright world outside the taxi as it continued the short ride on NW 21st Street to the airport concourse.

* * *

A helicopter clattered noisily over the hospital camp, then faded away buzzing like some magnified metal insect. In the tents on the wooded slopes of the mountain lived a small town's worth of health workers and their patients from the streets of Ercolano below. The hospital tents were growing in number as the number of infected citizens grew day by day. The hospital camp had now swallowed dozens of small tomato-growing market gardens and farms on the slopes of Vesuvius. In the distance, beyond the stunning blue sea over the Bay of Naples sprawled the city of Naples itself where poverty and crowding would make a fine breeding ground for the mosquitoes and the spreading of the malaria parasites they carried from person to person.

Maybe a thousand patients now lay on thin, canvas beds under mosquito nets that were too late, but might prevent the infected patients being reservoirs of infection for uninfected mosquitoes, alone in the tents that were clustered round the original Emergency Response Unit (ERU) that had been set up when the areas existing medical services became overwhelmed. Some recovered, but by and large they shivered and sweated, and raved and died. Every morning health workers flown in from the north of Italy and abroad ferried the new bodies to the flames that were burning downwind.

There was a blue smoky pall of despair mingled with the scent of fear that hung over the mountainside.

Dissociated, walking like an automaton, Dr Smyth wandered from tent to tent. Newly qualified that summer from medical school, Smyth had been unprepared for the sights he had endured in the last few days. He was suited up and smothered in insect repellent and couldn't remember when he had last slept. He saw some of his charges only once after they were evacuated from the town below in the shadow of the volcano. Others he saw a few times, but he was wholly unprepared for the unremitting savageness of the infection they were all fighting and the toll it was exacting. There was no treatment that worked. He could only support and watch. He felt impotent and humiliated.

One patient he had visited more than a few times, a young woman, who said nothing, but stared at him imploringly from out of dark brown, sunken eyes. Intravenous quinine had been ineffective. Intravenous fluids had reduced her gaunt, dehydrated look somewhat. He'd added some scarce N-acetyl-cysteine to try and reduce acidosis, but this had not worked.

Her renal function was deteriorating, and there were no longer any peritoneal dialysis kits. She was now desperately pale as many of her red cells had haemolysed leaving her anaemic. The nurses said that she had been fitting that morning. He had tried giving her some glucose. She lay flat, exhausted, unable to raise one finger. During the darkest part of the night she had told nurses she saw a shining man of silver at the bottom of her bed and that he was calling her to him. He diagnosed cerebral malaria.

As Smyth watched she closed her eyes and slipped into a coma.

He wandered out of the tent without comment to the nurses, stony-faced, and wondered that no-one seemed to even know the girl's name.

* * *

Power had flown from Miami to Lima and finally to Iquitos. The journey had taken him ten hours and he was so very, very tired that he could easily have slept standing up. By the time he reached Iquitos he hadn't the energy to expend any irritability by growling at airport employees. His eyes felt very heavy with sleep. Taxis appeared to be limited to motorised rickshaw-like conveyances in a short queue outside. Power dragged himself to the taxi rank and asked how much it would be to get to the hotel, "Cuanto a llevarme al Hotel Acosta?"

The reply was rapid and made no sense to him. The taxi driver repeated something involving the words 'nuevo' and 'sol', but Power wasn't very good at any language beyond English and regretted trying to launch any conversation in Spanish. He shrugged and merely said 'si', and hoping for the best, slumped back into the taxi, clutching his meagre luggage, which included McAdams's laptop.

The Hotel Acosta was in walking distance of the banks of the river Amazon and although functional to a Spartan degree, it was clean and quiet. Power must have checked in and been shown to his room, but in the morning, when he awoke he had no memory of having these events. He lay in his sheets under the mosquito net, listening to the sounds of the birds outside and lazily watching the moving light and shadow from the leaves of the trees outside on the white walls of his room. He thought of phoning Lynch, but wondered what hour it was in England and whether he would be waking the detective up. He settled on a brief text:

> In Peru – Iquitos. Hoping to visit research station later.
> Power.

He must have dropped off again, for when he awoke it was later in the day and the sun had climbed in the sky. He felt rested, hopeful and above all else, hungry. He showered and then pulled on blue cargo trousers, and a soft, white linen shirt. The small hotel was only three storeys high, and he made his way down the stairs to breakfast amongst palms and hibiscus on the terrace. His first awakening had been horribly early, and even now after his second sleep it was only early in the breakfast sitting. He was offered coffee and made his way to a refrigerated buffet where he collected some orange juice. He stared at a panoply of plates of ham and sausage; none of which was available to him as a vegetarian. His stomach rumbled in protest. Nearby on a hot plate were some tepid fried eggs and tortillas of egg and potato. He settled for these and some toast. The toaster seemed to have had a permanent 'feeble' setting enabled and it took four separate and depressingly slow trips on the metal conveyor belt inside the toaster for one slice of bread to acquire even a hint of brownness. Power munched his way through the breakfast with relish though and watched the other diners with inquisitive pleasure. He always was a people watcher.

The receptionist gave him a map of the small city and confidently explained the way to the tropical disease research station. Power set out on the street Sargento Lores with well-rested strides towards his goal and sat down an hour later in some shade he had found by the side of the road; lost, hot, dusty and perplexed. He had passed the crumbling facades of old rubber-mansions, once grand and now painted garishly and festooned with numerous families. He had got lost in a market and been assailed by unfamiliar smells from the street vendors. He had walked through stalls with clear plastic bags full of brightly coloured rainforest 'medicines' and potions. He had passed stalls piled high with hot peppers – red and yellow, or fresh fruit – mangoes, limes and melons. Everywhere was over-stimulating – a bright world of colour – shocking pinks, oranges and turquoises. In another quadrant of the market laughing women had called out to him and proffered giant snails, a thing that had looked like a skinned howler monkey, there were hacked crocodile tails, tortoises and possibly a pale armadillo. He felt nauseated. And the sights and smells haunted him even as he sat away from the market in the shade of a tree. He nursed the bag containing the laptop that he had brought along lest it be stolen from his room. A boy pushing a small, cafés-worth of goods in a glass-walled handcart along the street stopped by Power and made a sales pitch in the local language, not Spanish. Power looked up, uncomprehending. The boy smiled at him and spoke some English, with an American accent. "You are lost? Thirsty?" Power nodded, and the boy offered some juicy red watermelon, which Power gratefully handed over some cash for and slurped at the juice-filled cells of the melon. The boy watched Power thoughtfully. "Where are you looking for?" he asked.

"The naval research station on the road, Prolongacion Trujillo. It's a lab. Studies infections. Malaria. Fevers. You know?" Power didn't think the boy would know.

"Ah," the boy said. "The doctors. I will show you."

And with that Power followed the boy and his cart of bottles, melons, sweets, and corn chips. They rattled along; a caravan of cart, boy and man, for a few hundred yards and they stopped by a low, nineteen-seventies style concrete building, painted in white with a green metal roof.

"Here are the other doctors for you," said the boy grinning.

"Other doctors?" asked Power.

"You are a doctor too; I think."

"Well spotted," said Power as he tipped the boy. He asked

the boy the best way back to the hotel, and the boy laughed that Power had got so ridiculously lost. The hotel was very close, perhaps only a few hundred metres away. Power sighed and laughed at himself. "Thank you for your help. You are a better navigator and people watcher than I am."

There was a young secretary behind a sliding window. It took a few moments for Power to attract her attention. There weren't too many visitors at the research station. Eventually, Power caught her eye and she leapt up and hurried over to the window. There was a burst of Spanish that Power did not catch, and he introduced himself, in English.

"Good morning. I am Dr Carl Power. Do you speak English?"

"Yes, of course. How can I help you?"

"I wanted to know if you had a Dr Zuckerman here. He would probably be working on malaria. Dr Zuckerman? I've come a long way and need to speak with him." As he made his request, he noted that there was an unmistakable scowl growing on her face. "Is there something wrong?"

"Yes, we know Dr Zuckerman. And yes, he did some work for us on patients with malaria. Is he a friend of yours? A colleague?"

Power thought the right answer would be to say no. "I don't know him; I just need to speak with him."

"You can tell a man by the company he keeps. It is good you are not his friend. The Director fired him a week ago."

Power was crestfallen. She noticed his disappointment. "I know you have come a long way, but even if he doesn't work here, I can still tell you where he is. Where he always is. A bar. Drinking his liver to death."

"Ah," said Power. He felt desperate and wondered if his long journey had been futile.

"He is a lazy man. The other doctors had to dictate all his clinic letters. They complained to the Director when he came back from a field trip and when Zuckerman came to see the Director he was both late and drunk. He was told to clear his desk there and then."

"Is there any particular bar I should try?"

She looked at her watch. It was only ten forty-five. "He will be in the Calypso bar over the street. He doesn't walk far. He just lives in a room upstairs. He might have been a handsome man once, but drink has killed his soul."

Power looked through the doors into the shiny white labs beyond. He would have liked to have toured the station and learned more. He could see researchers wearing blue-green gowns, gloves and clear face masks by lab benches and wondered what they were working on. She watched him. She thought he was a polite, handsome man, quite unlike Zuckerman. "You can come back and have a tour, if you like," she offered. Power nodded.

"It's been while since I was in a lab . . . it was way back in medical school."

"They are busy, Dr Power, but I could show you, later." She smiled at him. "They are worried about the new type of malaria that's been found in Europe and other places. They are worried in case it reaches here. But you know what? I think before we go round you'd better go and talk to Zuckerman. He'll be too drunk if you leave it much longer."

Power thanked her, left the research station and negotiated his way across the street that thronged with taxi-bikes to the so-called Calypso bar. It was a two-storey brick building that opened downstairs on the street, spilling a few tables and chairs onto the pavement, under an awning. The bricks were part-stuccoed and painted in white and turquoise. A smiling parrot, painted on the stucco, leered down at Power from under the word 'Calypso' painted in neon orange.

As far as Power was aware Calypso originated in the West Indies, not South America and wondered if the bar would be as authentic as an Irish bar in New York.

There was no-one at the tables in the street, but inside the gloomy wooden interior sat a lone figure, in a red-checked shirt, hunched over a table, his back to the street. There was a distant sound of piped reggae music from some speakers over the bar. Some sounds of chickens and possibly piglets came from an open door at the back of the bar, by a small kitchen. A thin, grey-haired bartender with long hair in braids smiled at Power as he entered the shadows of the bar.

"Nada de beber señor?" Power looked confused. The bartender understood and said, "Anything to drink, sir?"

"Thank you, er, a Cusquena beer and whatever my friend here is having..." Power waved a hand towards the only other occupant of the bar.

Zuckerman looked up at Power from the table where he

slumped. "I'm not your friend, but I cannot refuse your charity. Who are you, sir?"

"I am Dr Power," he said, seating himself opposite Zuckerman. He could see the NAMRU 6 research station, the place that had dismissed the researcher opposite him, over Zuckerman's right shoulder. Power held out his hand to shake, but Zuckerman ignored it out of disdain or inebriation. "The receptionist said you'd be here."

The bartender placed a glass of ice-cold beer in front of Power and what looked like a whisky sour. "Cusquena and pisco sour." He offered Power a menu, which he took gratefully.

"When in Rome . . ." muttered Zuckerman, downing half of his drink in one gulp. He looked at Power. "What do you want?"

"I want to talk," said Power. "About McAdams." He scanned down the menu and turned to the barman. "Do you have anything . . . er . . . vegetarian? Vegetariano? Can you recommend anything? Me puede recomendar algo?"

"Si, Papa a la huancaina." Power nodded assent and wondered what he would get. He asked Zuckerman, "Want to join me? Have you eaten?"

Zuckerman laughed and indicated that only a refill would do. The barman understood perfectly. He'd been serving Zuckerman for weeks.

"Where are you living?" asked Power.

"Over the shop," said Zuckerman. "They chucked me out of the Research Centre's accommodation. I've got a room over the bar, now. It's ridiculously cheap and . . . so convenient." He sniggered at his own humour.

The barman put a plate of hard boiled eggs and boiled yellow potatoes in a creamy sauce in front of Power and also set down another glass of Pisco. This time Zuckerman held it thoughtfully, and did not swig it down. "So, you want to know about McAdams . . . how did you track me down?"

The potato dish was good, and Power was surprisingly hungry after his walk around the city. He took a few mouthfuls before he talked. "I wanted to know about McAdams. How he was with you? How you worked together? How he seemed to you? I had to do a report on him, as a psychiatrist. For the coroner, you understand." He looked at Zuckerman weighing him up. "I'm sorry; you did know he was dead?"

"I know all right. He sent me here. Convinced me it was for my safety. Then he goes and dies in an accident. Leaving me here. In the middle of fucking nowhere."

Power shook his head. "He saved your life. And his death was no accident."

"You know, Dr Power, when you live and work with a crazy person. You can kind of see things from their point of view. Be with them long enough you start to believe in their delusions. I believe you psychiatrists call it folie à deux."

"Yes, there is such a thing as *folie à deux*, but this was no delusion of Dr McAdams."

"I've had plenty of time to reflect, Dr Power. And I'll give you the fact that McAdams was very convincing. Convincing enough to even get me to give up my job at Howarth-Weaver and flee the country and start work at the edge of the fucking jungle." He swallowed a mouthful of spirits. "But it was a folie à deux or rather, with Dr Lloyd being involved as well, more of a folie à trois."

Power had finished his plate of food. He wondered if the growing disagreement with Zuckerman would inevitably lead to indigestion. He fixed his gaze on Zuckerman's eyes. "Dr McAdams had no mental illness. His suicide was faked. There was evidence of a struggle on the boat before he ended up in the water. When he sent you here, McAdams was saving your life. The police in England think he was murdered."

"I am sitting here. Sitting in the arsehole of the world, because of McAdams's paranoia, Dr Power. You're a psychiatrist. You should be able to see it for what it is."

Power decided to change tack. "What were you working on with McAdams? What did he think was so important that he was willing to risk himself to save?"

"A malaria drug, we called it Plasmosid. I did the clinical trials in Sudan, Yemen and Thailand. I always get the nicest places to work. But none as bad as here. It's okay if you like bushmeat – like gnawing the fucking trotters off an armadillo! I can't wait to get back home."

"Plasmosid might have been very useful, don't you think, considering the reports we're hearing on the news?"

Zuckerman nodded; he had to concede the point. "Malaria is one of the most contagious diseases, Dr Power. Have you ever heard of the BRN? The Basic Reproduction Number?"

The barman hovered at their elbow and Power ordered

two more drinks. He was keen to keep Zuckerman talking. "I'm a psychiatrist," said Power. "I share a medical background with you, but I'm not an infectious diseases expert."

Zuckerman sneered, "Surely, this is basic shit, even for a psychiatrist."

He was laughing at Power and decided to rub Power's nose in the puddle of his ignorance. "The BRN was devised by MacDonald in the nineteen-fifties. It's a measure of how many other new cases you can expect to follow on from a single, existing case of infection. So a case of measles, which is transmitted in an airborne way might generate 12-18 new cases. Other infections that require spread via bodily fluids are more difficult to transmit. One case of HIV might generate 2-5 new cases. A new case of Ebola might only generate 1-2 new cases.

"But – because malaria is transmitted by mosquitoes one case is amplified many, many fold. The BRN for malaria can be over 100 . . . because an infected human can be bitten many times by mosquitoes – think of them like flying needles – flying syringes – transmitting that one human's infected blood – over a range of many miles."

"So if we had Plasmosid and we were able to reduce that reservoir of infection in humans, it would help stop the spread. Can you help us get Plasmosid back? Dr Lloyd, Corinne, said it would take a year or more to get it back. She said that the company destroyed all your work. All the files they had that you'd left behind. All the data you collected in your field trials. Why did they do that?"

"You're asking a rhetorical question, Dr Power. I may be fucking drunk. But you're trying to get me on your side."

"It's not a question of sides, Dr Zuckerman. There are people dying. It's not theoretical. Your drug could have saved them."

"That's not my problem," slurred Zuckerman. "Being stuck in a forest hellhole is my problem."

"Do you know anything that might help? Anyway we could get the data back. Did McAdams leave something with you? A computer disk. A password? Anything?" Unconsciously, to reassure himself, Power put his hand on the bag he still had the laptop in.

"McAdams was mad. Paranoid. He wouldn't leave that kind of thing with me." Power understood then that McAdams wouldn't have left anything with Zuckerman for an entirely different reason. Zuckerman simply was not safe.

"Earlier you said something about going home," said Power. He had nearly finished his own beer and had yet to start on his second. He had lost count of the number of spirits Zuckerman had downed. Power started counting out notes as an interim payment for the meal and the drinks he had bought them. The barman was by his side in an instant, and the notes had gone. "What did you mean about going home?"

"I'm going home," Zuckerman sounded pleased with himself. "Today as a matter of fact. It's all sorted."

"Sorted with who?"

"The company," smiled Zuckerman. "They said they'd have me back any day. And Corinne. She can come back too. Two spies coming in from the cold. Only it's bloody hot in Raleigh and Peru . . . so that line doesn't work. Does it."

"McAdams was careful. Very careful. He gave you a cover here. And Corinne. He gave you both a cover story. So you couldn't be found. He paid for that." Power kept his voice very calm, but he was very angry. "And I think . . . it sounds like . . . you have told them where you are. And where Corinne is."

Zuckerman nodded. "And so would you. Would you stay here? Because of somebody else's delusion."

And then Power noticed something new in the space outside over Zuckerman's right shoulder. A taxi-bike had drawn up outside the Research Centre. And out of it stepped, with animal grace, the dark-haired figure of Cousins. He looked around briefly and drew a large valise from the back of the taxi bike, threw some coins at the taxi-biker and headed up the path to the reception of the Research Centre. Power realised he would not be touring the Research Centre after lunch and stood up.

"Thank you for the conversation, Dr Zuckerman, but I really must go. I'm taking a tour into the jungle." He wasn't, of course, but he knew Cousins would ask if Zuckerman mentioned him, which he would. Power also know that it would only be a few seconds before Cousins was sent over to the bar to find Zuckerman by the research centre's receptionist.

Zuckerman looked up from his drink, confused at the abrupt end to the conversation. Power was nowhere to be seen. Zuckerman looked over his shoulder into the street, but Power was gone.

NINE

Power had left the bar by the rear, across a courtyard filled with dirt and chickens and pigs. The barman who was now feeding the chickens in the yard looked after him bemused. Power's fear lent his language skills some urgency and he stammered, "Yo no estaba aquí", and pushed more money into the surprised man's hands.

And then he ran. He ran like he had never done before. He pelted down alleys until he got onto the route back to the hotel that the boy had shown him. He arrived in the lobby both breathless and covered in rivulets of sweat. The receptionist stared at the beetroot red doctor in some concern, "Are you all right?"

"A fast taxi to the airport please, quick as you can, it's urgent." The receptionist picked up the phone and started dialling. Power patted his pockets to make sure he had his wallet, passport, phone and the laptop. He had decided to leave any other luggage to travel as swiftly as he could. He had no intention of returning to his room and packing if he could help it. How much time did he have before Cousins picked up his trail? The receptionist put down the phone. "And can you make up my bill too, please?"

Sensing Power's panic, the receptionist calmly added up the bill and presented it to him then watched as Power started scattering high value Nuevo Sol notes onto the counter.

"That's more than enough, Doctor . . ."

"Take it, take it, "Power muttered distractedly looking around for the taxi.

"It won't be long, Doctor." And sure enough a Moto taxi – a three wheeled motorbike taxi drove up to the reception area.

Power let out an expletive and turned to the receptionist. "Isn't there anything faster?"

"That's what we have. It will just take fifteen minutes to the airport."

"Okay, okay, I'm sorry." And swearing again at how ridiculous the transport seemed to him, Power scrambled in the back, urging the need for speed to the taxi driver, and they sped off.

It was now early afternoon and Power knew there was only a few flights a day out of Iquitos to Lima. If he was lucky, he could find a seat on the flight later that afternoon. If only he could get there on time. The streets were packed with goats, bicycles and pedal bike taxis. Power's Moto taxi driver did his best, but he could feel the frustration of Power building up behind him in the taxi seat. Every now and then there were explosions of panicked annoyance from Power as they negotiated their way in a stop-start manner towards the airport. Power kept turning round; he imagined Cousins just behind them or perhaps overtaking them on a short-cut and getting to the airport ahead of him.

At the airport, there was further alarm for Power as the ticket salesman first of all advised Power that the flight was fully booked, then turned up a single seat that someone had just cancelled. Then Power's credit card would not work, having been disowned by the bank for being used in South America. A second card did go through and clutching his ticket and the laptop tightly, Power made for the departure gates, all the time looking over his shoulder.

Only two hours later, as he ducked into the threadbare anonymity of a cash-only downtown hotel in Lima, did Power begin to relax a little. Even so, he kept periodically looking out of his first-floor window onto the street below. He picked up his mobile. It would be very late in the UK, but he needed to speak to someone. He had a service from a local provider and dialled Lynch's number. Far away, in Chester, Lynch's phone began to ring.

A sleepy sounding Superintendent Lynch answered, "Lynch here, who's there please?"

"Its Carl."

"Carl!" His sleepiness evaporated. "Where are you?"

"A rather dingy hotel in Lima. I've only got limited battery life. I left my charger in my last hotel. I had to run and fly out of Iquitos in a hurry."

"Why? Are you all right?"

"A bit shaken. Just calming down. Cousins was there. He arrived there, just as I was talking to Zuckerman. He didn't see me, but I felt frightened. It was a surprise seeing him there. I had to run. I've got no clothes. I'll have to get some tomorrow, and I will need to fly out of Lima."

"Do you need help?"

"The bank stopped my card. Only one is working. Can you

fix things?" Power told him his bank details. Lynch agreed to intercede. Power needed a reliable supply of money.

"You should come home," said Lynch. "I've been praying for your safety. You've done enough. Come home now."

"I can't stop now," said Power. "There's so much riding on this. The drug Plasmosid could save lives. We have to get it back somehow. I have arranged to see Marianne Howarth-Weaver – I'm hoping she will help."

"She's more than likely part of the problem," said Lynch.

"I'm hoping otherwise," said Power. "That she can undo what her company has done."

"Was Zuckerman any help?"

"Worse than none. McAdams saved him – just like he saved Dr Lloyd – but he needn't have bothered with Zuckerman. Zuckerman doesn't believe that McAdams was killed. He has swallowed the company line. He hates where McAdams hid him, hates the memory of McAdams and is busily drinking himself into an early grave there. He thinks that he has done a deal with the company and is going to be brought back into the fold. As far as Zuckerman was concerned McAdams's self-sacrifice was a waste . . . And Andrew?"

"Yes?"

"It's logical to assume, if Zuckerman didn't feel he was at risk from the company . . . that he didn't respect the safety of Dr Lloyd. Didn't keep her secrets safe. I'm worried that he betrayed her to Cousins. Zuckerman is a walking security risk. And at the moment Lloyd is our only chance to get the drug back. She might take a year or so, but I think she could do it if we got her out and supported her." Power had more to say. About the lives that could be saved if the drug were available, but he was suddenly aware that he was talking into nothing. The battery had died. It would be tomorrow before he could re-charge. He hoped that Lynch had heard enough and had understood. Power sank back onto the bed and slept.

* * *

The North Carolina police had two cars parked outside the two-storey buildings where the University housed its research fellows and their families. Yellow tape with "Crime Scene Do Not Enter" cordoned off the yard in front of the steps that led up to Dr Lloyd's flat. Badged officers in fawn trousers and black shirts milled about by their cars. Only white-suited crime scene investigators were allowed upstairs. They paid close attention to the bottles of pills that had been strewn about the bed, which the body of Corrine Lloyd had been found in.

Once her death had been confirmed, and evidence collected, a private ambulance had been summoned to take her away to the N.C. Office of the Chief Medical Examiner.

It had been Superintendent Lynch who had triggered the early morning call by the N.C. Police department to the University. The University had confirmed that Corinne had not been into work for several days. She had returned to the University labs after her meeting with Power. She had seemed busy and happy after that meeting. She stayed late and wrote up the results of her day's researches. Next day she had not showed for work.

After the discovery the N.C. Police were eager to contact Superintendent Lynch in England to ask just what had led to his concerns that Corinne was in imminent danger.

* * *

In the early light of dawn, the female mosquito happened to chance its flight into the warm bedroom of the farmer's wife. She lay under a mound of knitted blankets and cotton sheets near the veranda of the bungalow in Patna. She had been shivering for most of the night with malaria and was tired. Her arm lolled out of the sheets, and so the mosquito settled on her forearm and drank its blood meal. Later that day or the next the newly infected mosquito would move on to feed on the occupant of the bungalow on the neighbouring farm nearby and transfer some of the cargo of falciparum parasites from its belly to the next human victim.

Outside on the goat farm they owned, the goats roamed hungrily and noisily in their pens. They protested as their bellies rumbled. It had been days since the farmer or his wife had been well enough to feed them.

* * *

The next morning Power had rejected the sad breakfast offerings of the hotel and took off into Lima to find a charger for his phone. A nearby cyber café – Cinco Continentes – had recharging facilities. Power was alternately checking his email, drinking coffee and munching a croissant when Lynch's text came through.

> Dear Carl – I triggered a search of Dr Lloyd's home by the N.C. police. Sad to report Dr Lloyd has been found dead. Foul play suspected. Suggest you abort trip to see CEO and come home safe.

Power stared into space. His chances of restoring the work on Plasmosid had just disappeared far away into the fog. The prospect had been distant enough when Corinne Lloyd had been alive. She had estimated a year to restore the drug even with her advanced knowledge. Now her mind and memories had been erased. All that was left of the original team was the spirit-sodden Dr Zuckerman and Power wouldn't bet on him as a starter to re-create the drug.

He texted Lynch back,

> Thank you for your thoughts. No option but to go on.
> Carl.

TEN

Cousins had hired a Land Rover to get them to the edge of the rainforest. They were on the very edge of a clearing and ahead of them was dense green forest.

The unearthly sound of howler monkeys sounded hideous to Zuckerman.

"I can't believe you want to go in there," said Zuckerman.

"Oh, I couldn't come all this way and not go into the forest. The opportunity to see the wildlife – monkeys, sloths, birds, inside there are lagoons too. I believe that it's beautiful. Haven't you been in there?"

"We should have a guide," said Zuckerman weakly.

"I'm not going far," said Cousins. "A few hours in there is all I want. Then I can send you home."

Zuckerman was sitting on the open tailgate of the Landy, pulling on his boots and tucking his trousers into his socks. "Best to cover up. Put plenty of repellent on."

"I will follow the expert's example," said Cousins, without a shred of irony in his voice. "Tell me, Marcus. How did Dr Power seem? What did he want to know?"

Zuckerman could hardly remember. Nowadays when he'd been drinking, he often did not recall the day before. "I don't know. He seemed a bit agitated. A bit determined. Focused."

"Determined. Yes, he must be. To follow you across the

other side of the world. That's motivated. But what did he want? Do try and remember, please."

"He wanted to know all about the Plasmosid project. If it could be re-created."

"And what did you tell him?" Cousins asked, and having seen Zuckerman's shake of his head, swallowed down his frustration and contempt for the man. "Do try, there's a good chap . . ." Cousins had started his walk into the forest. He stepped into the shadow under the trees. Zuckerman followed him, shrugging a rucksack of food and water bottles onto his back, and stepping himself into the humid and noisy gloom that teemed with life.

"I think I would have said that only McAdams had the data."

"And what did Power say about McAdams? Did I tell you that I met him at poor Dr McAdams's inquest? He came across as some kind of a conspiracy nerd . . ."

"He seemed hooked on the idea that McAdams didn't kill himself."

"Absurd," said Cousins. "McAdams was a deranged man. Don't you think?"

"Absolutely," said Zuckerman. It was dim under the leaf canopy. Occasional shafts of light penetrated the darkness. There was the sound of trickling water. The smell of the steamy soil. "I can't believe that I let him send me to this place." He looked about the forest with distaste.

"Its okay, Marcus. I'm sending you home."

The taser hit Zuckerman in his chest. The two metal

contacts had hooked into him just below his ribcage and 6 kV of electricity felled him in an instant.

Cousins stepped over to Zuckerman's unconscious body and pulled out a pre-filled injection pen. He pushed the needle into Zuckerman's right deltoid muscle and squeezed the trigger. 200mg of suxamethonium flowed into his bloodstream. Complete muscular relaxation followed. The drug's actions, which would include respiratory paralysis would last for up to six minutes. Like any normal human being, Dr Zuckerman would not survive this.

Cousins checked the scene around Zuckerman's body. He believed that he had removed all traces of himself. The drug would not be detected, but then the forest would cover any trace of the crime, digesting Zuckerman's body within days. And Cousins doubted that any human would venture near in weeks or even months.

Leaving Zuckerman behind, Cousins followed the GPS signal back to the Landy. He swigged a bottle of water by the side of the vehicle and then, firing up the engine, set off back down the trail towards the airport.

* * *

There was always a queue outside the Brooklyn diner on West 57th. There was always a table screened off for Jared Howarth-Weaver. No matter how long the queue was, no matter how empty the booth was, Jared had paid for the booth and empty the booth would remain.

When Jared was in town he would use it most days. Today he was reading the *Wall Street Journal* and an article about the rise and rise of Howarth-Weaver shares. Howarth-Weaver owned the worldwide patent on the only effective insecticide against the resistant *Anopheles* mosquito the company had itself introduced into the wild. Since July Jared's shares and, accordingly, his personal fortune had trebled in value. He had celebrated with a larger breakfast than normal and was finishing his third cup of coffee when Cousins flew into the diner, made his way up to the booth and slid along the bench opposite Jared.

Jared looked up from his paper. "I see Princess Diana died in a tunnel in Paris last week. Tell me, do you feel any grief, as an Englishman?"

"None."

"Well, that does not surprise me about you." Jared fixed his gaze on Cousins. Cousins looked calm and imperturbable, and was immaculately dressed, as ever, in black. "How are things? I must report to my brother later, and he will want good news, as ever."

"Well, the news is positive, overall."

A waitress lingered by the table to see if there was an order for Cousins, but Jared waved her away, with the comment, "He'll eat on his own time."

When she had gone, Jared refined his question. "Specifically, what is 'positive'".

"I have concluded business in Raleigh and Iquitos. So, to summarise, all the files and records of the chemistry, development and trials of Plasmosid are destroyed. The team that worked on Plasmosid is gone."

"'And so even the memory of the drug has disappeared, like a dream that once dreamt is now forgot.'" Jared chuckled. "Well done; the way is clear then?"

"Not quite," said Cousins. "Do you recall that I mentioned a Dr Power? He was at the inquest of Dr McAdams. He didn't believe that McAdams killed himself. I didn't consider him a significant opponent then, but he has demonstrated a form of persistence that makes him an annoyance."

"That you mention him to me a second time, would suggest that Dr Power is more than an 'annoyance'. What has he done?"

"He was there, in Raleigh, and in Iquitos."

Jared frowned, and his gaze seemed more of a glare. "What is he, police? What does he know? What does he want?"

Cousins knew that Jared would scent any equivocation or minimisation. "He was asking questions of Lloyd and Zuckerman, about how to re-create the drug. Power got nowhere of course. He's not able to recreate it himself. He's a psychiatrist. But he has a friend, Superintendent Lynch. And Lynch tipped off the police about Corinne Lloyd. I only just got out of Raleigh before a Federal bulletin was put out to all the airports about my passport. I'm under an earlier identity now."

Jared raised his eyebrows. "How many identities have you got? And am I talking to the real Mr Cousins? "

"Never mind. You call me. I respond, don't I?"

"You sound rattled, Mr Cousins. I don't like that."

"Well, maybe it's your turn to be rattled, Mr Howarth-Weaver. Dr Power has an appointment with your sister Marianne."

But Jared did not give Cousins the pleasure of seeing him discomforted. He looked away to the view outside the diner. "There's an exhibition on over the road. I want to be there in ten minutes, so let's wrap this up. Firstly we agreed that when the new strain had taken hold, and there was a demand for our insecticide that there would be a distribution of rewards. Those rewards have been transferred to your Swiss account for you to distribute to your agents who helped us. I don't want to know who they are. Ever. If they become talkative now or in the future, you know what to do.

"Secondly, you underestimated Dr Power. That displeases me, because you were not alert to the threat he presents to us all. I must ask that you do not underestimate him again.

"Thirdly, and this is most regrettable. It concerns our sister. I'm not sure if you have any siblings?" Cousins shook his head. "The price is almost too much to bear, but it is a matter that my brother and I have foreseen and discussed. The future direction of the firm will be safer in my brother and my hands. As the stock price clearly shows. Years of slow decline under Marianne's tutelage reversed handsomely with just one initiative of ours. Marianne represents a very real and unacceptable threat to the company's future direction and profit. Further funds will be transferred on completion . . ."

"And you would like me to act?"

Jared was standing and buttoning up his jacket. There was an almost imperceptible nod, and with that he left the diner, passing the hungry queue outside. He crossed the road to the gallery as Cousins too slipped out of the front door. The booth that they both left went back to its ever-empty existence.

In the Marlborough Gallery across the road, Jared rounded a corner away from the plate glass windows and when he knew that Cousins could no longer see him sought a bench and slumped down onto it. Around him hung the art from their Summer Exhibition. A nearby member of staff recognised him as one of its wealthiest patrons and shimmered over. "Mr Howarth-Weaver, I'm so pleased to welcome you back. Can I offer you a little refreshment? Some Champagne?"

Jared looked around distractedly. "Do you have a little brandy, please?" As the member of staff drifted away, Jared looked at his shaking hand. He groaned so loud that people in the gallery turned to look at him. He waved off their offers of assistance. The brandy arrived, and he sipped it, eyes closed to block out his surroundings. When he felt a little revived, he held his hand out again. The tremor was subsiding. He hadn't wanted Cousins to see any of this. He tried to steady his breathing and subdue the panic in his chest. It isn't every day you order the death of your sister. He thought of her as a child, his big sister. Picking him up when he fell off the ottoman and the head of the stairs. Making lemon squash from Sicilian lemons in the Summer. Scolding him when he disturbed their father when he banged his drum outside a meeting in the study. Always in the goddamn way when he grew up. Still, it wasn't too late to summon Cousins back. It was still possible . . . Jared shuddered, he suddenly felt so cold and small, and old.

* * *

Power was in his room at the Royal York Hotel in Toronto under an assumed name, set up by Lynch. He was lying back on the vast bed watching a re-run of an interview with Tony Blair on the BBC World Service. In the interview from over a week ago, Blair was standing outside a church and expounding on his grief. "You know . . . people everywhere, not just here in Britain but everywhere, they kept faith with Princess Diana; they liked her, they loved her, they regarded her as one of the people. She was the people's princess, and that's how she will stay, how she will remain in our hearts and in our memories forever.

"She seemed full of happiness, full of life, she was great fun to be with and she was an unusual but a really warm character and personality and I will remember her personally with very great affection. I think the whole country will remember her with the deepest affection and love, and that is why our grief is so deep today."

Power nearly switched off in revulsion. Power mourned the Princess in his own way, but something about Blair's manner seemed inherently fake and Power had always felt nauseated by him. He put the remote control down however, as the next report was headlined 'Malaria in Barcelona'.

A young reporter with long hair and brown almond eyes

stared out of the screen at Power. Behind her was the main entrance of the University Hospital Clínic de Barcelona. "A new strain of mosquito and a new resistant strain of *Plasmodium* have combined into a perfect storm of an epidemic that is sweeping not only traditional malaria areas in Africa and Asia, but also Southern Europe. The new mosquito is hardier than previous strains and able to survive further north and south than the equator. The new strain of a parasite carried by the mosquito is resistant to conventional drugs. The only safeguards that can be used are the old-fashioned ones of mosquito nets, water management and a remarkable brand new insecticide that is selling so fast it is becoming scarce and the factories cannot keep up with demand. The share price of its manufacturer, Howarth-Weaver has quadrupled over recent days. Here at the main hospital in Barcelona there are over two hundred new cases of malaria this week alone. Only a few survive. The medical advice is cover up, use insect repellents, sleep under nets, avoid public places at dawn and dusk and treat standing water. If you have been abroad in an affected area and feel unwell, contact your doctor as soon as possible."

Power groaned and switched on McAdams's laptop and tried, for another half an hour, to crack the password, and gave up, dispirited. Frustrated, he put the laptop away again, took a gin and tonic from the minibar and nursing his glass, watched the bright city lights of Toronto against the velvet black night of early September.

ELEVEN

Power had killed time in Toronto with coffee, art galleries, a trip up the CN Tower, even sat through a baseball match with the BlueJays at the SkyDome. He had liked the easy atmosphere but was amazed at the crowd's lack of concentration on the game. He killed time until his meeting. He had pinned all his hopes on this.

Marianne Howarth-Weaver, the Howarth-Weaver Chief Executive, lived on the Toronto Islands. The Islands sit offshore in Lake Ontario and have two views – the vast blue lake – so big that the other side cannot be seen with the naked eye – or the Toronto skyline. The Islands are alluvial deposits from the erosion of an escarpment, the Scarborough Bluffs.

Only a hundred or so families live on the Islands in mainly small clapboard houses. In the nineteen-fifties, the Howarth-Weaver family had bought three and demolished them to build the largest house on the islands overlooking a west-facing bay on Ward's Island. There had been several attempts over the years to clear private householders off the Islands to enlarge the successful public pleasure park. Thousands of visitors came over on ferries every day during the summer and strolled or biked over the islands, which were linked by boardwalks. Cars are banned on the islands, but that only adds to their charm. Visitors hire bicycles, tandems, tricycles or quadricycles. Some hire canoes or pedal boats. Marianne had always fought to retain her foothold, her family's home, on the islands. She had hoped to pass it down to her children, but there were none. When she died, she thought she might bequeath the house to her sole nephew or a charity.

She used the house as a retreat from the business. At times, it felt as if her father was still with her in that house on the Island. Sipping coffee, reading some papers. Joking in his own way. He would escape from their mother in a boat, and fish. Sometimes he would take her and they would sit side by side and he would lecture her on human nature, and how to 'keep a hold of your money, except for the best of causes, acos there's plenty and more that'd have it off ye'. He spoke of money like a liquid; that had to be channelled to where it would do the most good either for you or others. He'd even told her about a secret machine at the Bank of England that modelled the economy using water, flowing between tanks, along pipes mimicking the flow of money in taxes, investments and exports. She hadn't believed him, because it sounded so ramshackle, but when she was older learned that her father had been correct. And here she was herself on the island, surrounded by water, and absolutely governed by it. When it was winter and froze, there was often no way out. She kind of liked that, and had resented it one icy day when the lake had frozen around the Islands and she had phoned her secretary to cancel her meetings to be told that she was so vital that they would send a helicopter for her. She had sometimes wondered whether the Bank of England's model economy had ever frozen over. Maybe it would be a bad sign, like the doom associated with Ravens leaving the Tower of London.

That morning Marianne Howarth-Weaver had enjoyed a leisurely shower and taken coffee on the veranda overlooking the bay whilst reading *Alias Grace*, a novel by Margaret Atwood. She had tried to build a day at home without the distractions of running an international corporation, but it was a fight to get her own time. The afternoon would be filled with painting, and the evening filled with a game of Bridge with some of her oldest friends.

She had managed to keep up with her school and University friends. Three of them would arrive that evening and stay over in the house by the lake. One had an art foundation for disadvantaged children that Marianne supported, another was a Ph.D. supervisor at the University and another a genteel supporter of animal rights. Marianne relished her time away from the office. Somehow these days the office reminded her of her family - her late, very acquisitive mother and her two equally competitive and ever-dissatisfied brothers. At first the office had reminded her of her father, of his ideals and his vision for her and the future. After her father had died, it had been a struggle to steer the company in any direction that her brothers disapproved of. And they tended to disapprove of a lot. They disapproved of donations to environmental charities, to the creation of educational foundations and her endless patronage of Universities. "No-one likes a do-gooder," Michael kept saying. Jared always snorted derisively, "It's no good trying to buy a place in heaven anymore. Even the bishops admit they're only in it for the money."

At blessedly rare committee meetings with her brothers, she would ask, to their jeers, "Don't you think that the universe rewards good deeds?"

She recalled when, early in his twenties and early on in his time in Africa, Michael had become a fervent advocate for political change. And when Jared had been a student in the early sixties and taken part in sit-ins against Vietnam and for human rights. If these had been flowerings of conscience, then the flowering season had been very short and from their twenties onwards both brothers had been focused by their widowed mother on making profit. She had always thought them a bit rash and when they were small had followed them around outside advising caution and safety to their great irritation. She remembered their mother, reclining inside the house on a sofa, calling out to her, "Leave them alone Marianne. Boys will be boys and if they get hurt, Marianne, well they will learn not to do it again."

"But the water, mother! They could drown."

"You can't mollycoddle them all their lives, Marianne. Let them be."

Lost in her memories, Marianne happened to catch sight of the grandfather clock in the hall. Nearly time to meet the doctor. What was his name? She looked at her diary for the day; "Dr Power – lunch". She wondered what he was like and what he wanted and why she had allowed herself to see him so close to home.

She washed her face and hands, adjusted her make up and dress in the mirror and left the house, locking it carefully behind her. The day trippers who were ferried to the Islands sometimes wandered a little too much.

Outside it was still. A late Summer's day. She checked she had money in her purse and slipped it back into her handbag. She wouldn't need any money. She was well known at the Rectory – the local Island restaurant and her credit was excellent, but she liked the reassurance of being able to pay.

She walked to the restaurant along the narrow, tree-lined paths that wound between the houses. In the far distance, some tourists pedalling a quadricycle had become stuck on a too-narrow bridge between the islands. She was tempted to smile at their predicament, but thought this too cruel.

The white, stucco walled, green roofed Rectory restaurant had once been the home of the priest in charge of the church on the Islands. Now the Rectory was a bistro with a bar indoors and a patio overlooking Lake Ontario. Green painted, iron tables with iron trellis chairs were scattered over the patio. Trees and shrubs clustered around the patio.

As Marianne approached the patio area the manageress, Aileen, came out especially to greet her. "Ms Howarth-Weaver. How nice to see you, I'm so pleased you are booked with us today." Aileen was a tall, slim woman in her late twenties. Sometimes she looked rather drawn, and Marianne wondered if she was bordering on anorexic.

"Yes, yes, a light lunch. Meeting someone new, a Dr Power."

"Oh yes, he's arrived already. He's having a drink in the bar."

"I see. What's he like?"

"Very handsome. Quiet. English. Will you want your usual table on the patio?"

Marianne nodded. There were only a few diners as yet. It was early. A family of three and an elderly couple. The family's sulky daughter stared at Marianne in a disagreeable way. Beyond the café, on the green, Marianne noticed a man in a grey hoodie throwing a Frisbee for a dog. "Later, I wonder Aileen, could you arrange for some food to be brought over to the house? I'm having a Bridge four."

"Of course," said Aileen. "I'll put it on your account. What would you like, please?"

"Oh, some canapés. I'll leave it to you. Salmon, prawns. That sort of thing. And some nacho chips, salsa and guacamole. They're good to nibble on as you play cards."

"I'll bring it over myself. Round five p.m.?"

"Thank you, Aileen. I'll go to the table now. Will you go and ask Dr Power to join me, please?" She watched the ever-agreeable Aileen go into the Rectory and made her way through the tables to her favourite place, a round table set for two under a green awning by the white wall of the property.

She sat down and noted that the man in the grey hoodie who had been playing with the dog had seemingly divested himself of both dog and Frisbee and was standing staring out over the parkland, his back to her. She wondered where his dog had gone.

"Good afternoon," said Dr Power. A deep, smooth and urbane voice, Marianne thought. He had appeared silently by the table and was holding out his hand. His grip was firm, dry and warm, and he smiled easily. He was a tall man who sat down opposite her with an assuredness that spoke of a certain degree of confidence and worldliness. He took off his sunglasses and looked at her. His eyes were warm. She noted some laughter lines around his eyes. He smiled. "Thank you for meeting me. I like this place." A waitress had followed him and placed his drink, a Canadian Sauvignon Blanc, on the table in front of him. "Would you like a drink? Can I order you one?" He offered.

"Yes please, but I am treating you to lunch Dr Power, so please forget about picking up the tab. What are you drinking?"

"A Sauvignon Blanc from the Creekside Winery – I like to try local produce, and the restaurant told me that this is brand new. They're trying it out."

"Then I'll try a glass too," she nodded to the waitress who stood at Power's shoulder, and she drifted off to the bar for Marianne. "I've not tried many Canadian wines to be fair, considering I spend most of my time here. Have you ever tried Ice Wine, Dr Power?"

"No, what's that please?"

"It's a sweet wine, good with dessert. We might try some later. It's made from grapes harvested when they are frozen, so it makes a concentrated juice."

"I'd like to try it. Do you live here then? On the Islands? I noticed some houses. I came over on the ferry this morning and walked around the Islands a bit."

"I'm lucky enough to be a resident. You can't buy a property here for love nor money, but my Daddy built a family home here many years ago, and he passed it on. Then we had a dreadful fight trying to hang on to it. They wanted to clear the Islands of homes. Can you imagine? We fought it with lawyers all the way to the top and in the end – only a few years ago – the Government passed an Act, which enabled us to purchase 99-year land leases and get some permanence."

"I expect you can pass it on to your children?"

"Oh, I have no children Dr Power. Maybe a nephew might inherit, but he's a bit of a rebel. Where do you come from?"

"I am from Cheshire, from a village called Alderley Edge."

"Well, we are a long way from there, but you might be surprised to hear that I know Alderley Edge. I read a book called the *Weird Stone*, or something about Merlin I think. I read it when it came out – when I was a child. That's about Alderley Edge isn't it?" Power nodded. "I loved that book, magical stuff," she said.

"*The Weirdstone of Brisingamen*, by Alan Garner. My house is right by the Edge."

A waitress handed them some menus. "The menu is a short one, and nothing fancy. But I like this place. It sounds like you love your village too?" She scanned the menu to see if there were any changes, but she knew it backwards. "I was in Allminster earlier this year actually. That wouldn't be too far away, would it? I was bestowing a Howarth-Weaver Grant on the University there. I remember I had a picture taken with a bust of Mr Gladstone, the Prime Minister to Queen Victoria, on the campus. They said he founded the place. I thought he looked very stern. My brothers kicked up such a fuss about the Grant. Some people disapprove of anything that isn't pure profit. But if you can do some good, and it's all tax deductible, somehow, why not?" She realised she had perhaps said too much, and wondered what it was about Dr Power that made such confidences possible. "What kind of a doctor are you?"

"I'm a psychiatrist," he said, and was surprised when she laughed.

"Forgive me, that explains why you are such a good listener." The waitress had re-appeared. "What will you have Dr Power?"

Power looked up from the menu at the young waitress, "Thank you, I'll have the mixed organic greens starter then the Pizza Giardiniera, please."

"And I will have the Char-grilled Calamari and then Pancetta, Kale & Oka Cheese Omelette, please." She handed her menu over to the waitress after she had written the orders down. Once she had left Marianne rested her elbows on the table and steepling the fingers of her hands together, looked over the tips of her fingers at Power. "Now, Dr Power, you've travelled thousands of miles to speak to me, and you have more to say to me than a polite lunchtime conversation, very nice though this is."

"Yes, you're right, of course. It's about malaria."

"I hope that won't cause a bad atmosphere between us."

Power graced the joke with a small smile, but the gravity of his intended message made his sense of humour somewhat inhibited. She sensed this, "I can see that this is no laughing matter you visit me with."

"I would rather not be the bearer of bad tidings," said Power, looking down at the promising salad that had been placed before him. A waitress was placing additional cutlery for him, including a sharp pizza knife.

"Oh," said Marianne, noting that however bad the tidings, Dr Power's appetite seemed to have been retained. "I know the recent outbreaks of malaria have been terrible news. Dreadful of course. But the malaria has been good news for Howarth-Weaver – we've been able to supply a solution, the only insecticide that works, thankfully. What is so bad about that?"

Power looked up at her trying to size up just how much Marianne knew, and consequently how much he could trust her. "Is the new insecticide your own project? Something you've masterminded?"

"Indeed no, it's Michael's project. Michael is my brother. And the project is Michael's or at least that's what he tells me. He would take the credit, and of course always leaves my other brother, Jared, to take the blame. He always has. So Jared might conceivably have done some, or all, of the work. Michael spent a long time in Africa. He saw what malaria can do when he was there, of course. My father would have been proud of Michael, at last."

"They didn't get on?"

"No generation of Howarth-Weaver men gets on with the previous generation of Howarth-Weaver men. It's a family tradition. Look, Dr Power, are you a reporter? You seem to be able to get me to talk, and if this goes into print it will be very damaging. If you are a reporter, we must end with the starter I am afraid."

"I am not a reporter. I really am a doctor. I need your help, but it's important that you hear me out. I sense that it might not be easy stuff to listen to though, so please forgive me."

As the plates were being cleared away, Power paused. Marianne took the opportunity to order another two glasses of wine for her and Power. On the tables around them, diners came and went, but for Marianne she felt as if time had crawled to a halt. "I'm beyond intrigued Dr Power, please tell me, as swiftly and gently as you can what this is about?"

"Let me say that I appreciate that your company is vast. Global. And that if someone wanted to hide something from you, in that company, well I guess they could." Power hoped that was the case. He read Marianne as a reasonably sincere individual. "And I appreciate that your new insecticide is a life saver, in the circumstances. And I am sure that the company's profits from the insecticide will have been earned from your point of view. But from another point of view, if there was something that had been hidden from you, well I hope you might view things in a different light, and seek to redress things. To restore the balance." The main course had arrived, and Marianne toyed with her plate thoughtfully. Power used the wickedly sharp pizza knife to cut himself a slice.

He went on, "The insecticide option earns more than other options because it needs to be applied everywhere – on the walls, on floors, on the eaves of a house, around pools, on nets, and re-applied every few months. So it will earn billions. Every year."

"You said it earned more than other options. There aren't any other options, Dr Power."

"There were. There were other options. And that's my point, Marianne. That's where we need you. The reason I've come here is that I'm begging for your help."

"I would help if I could, naturally, but I really don't know."

And Power saw she really did not know what had been happening under her nose. "There was a drug, called Plasmosid, which was effective in this kind of malaria. Plasmosid was developed, manufactured and trialled by your company."

"No – that can't be right. I'd know about that – the product stream . . ." she looked at Power. He was earnest. "Are you sure?"

"It was a small team in the UK. The man who supervised the project was Dr McAdams. I have met the rest of his team, Drs Lloyd and Zuckerman. The drug was ready. But now, all traces of the project have gone." She frowned at his words. "As far as I can tell, the drug is no more. And I am begging you to try and get it back. If there's any way . . ."

She raised her palm for silence. "Dr Power. I am . . . struggling with this. It's a lot to take in. Until we met today, I had no inkling of any malaria drug, successful or not. I can't see that I wouldn't know about it. Although every pharmaceutical company has its own espionage and counterespionage division . . ."

"I don't think that you were meant to know. I don't think that I am meant to know about it. It would complicate things if people knew. You have a product that works – an insecticide – and it will make a huge profit because there's nothing else to combat this new strain. But if there were a drug, well then it would be a neater solution. You treat the patient once. You reduce the pool of disease. It doesn't get passed on. It's cheaper then forever applying the insecticide. You'd make less profit."

Marianne was pale. "Somebody took a decision. They weighed the two products in the balance. And one had to go"

"And it had to go completely. No traces left."

"You mentioned a team. We need to talk to them. Restore the project."

"Marianne, I'm sorry. The people who have eliminated the drug and the records of the project have been very thorough indeed. My involvement in all of this began when I was asked to do a report for the coroner on Dr McAdams. It was made to look like an overdose. And Dr Lloyd is dead too. The police tell me that Dr Zuckerman has not been seen for days."

"I can see you are genuine, Dr Power, but you must forgive me. This news is a little difficult to take in. I'm struggling to keep up with what you are saying. You start out, the day is arranged and going to plan, I was looking forward to lunch with you and then bridge with some friends . . . you don't expect these sudden swerves . . ."

Power paused. He and Lynch now fully suspected that the outbreaks of malaria had been as contrived as the marketing of the insecticide, and the ablation of the Plasmosid. Looking at Marianne now, he wondered if it was reasonable to unload the full scope of his fears onto her. The magnitude of his revelations might be too much to bear at once. He could see she was struggling to process what he had already said. And she had yet to work out the ramifications for her and her company. She was getting there though,

Marianne went on, "There would be a terrible price to pay . . . in lives lost . . . if the world was denied a drug that worked against treatment-resistant malaria. I'd ask who would do such a thing . . . who could keep all this from me . . . but I'm afraid to know."

"It sounds like you know," said Power.

"Yes. Unfortunately, I think I do, and you can't appreciate how disappointed I am. How let down? How used I feel? My father's company. My father stressed the importance . . . of sticking to our ethical principles . . . and now they have destroyed its heart, and perverted it from the core . . . Forgive me, Dr Power. I feel a little exposed here . . ." He could see that she was crying.

"There is some more that I think you may need to consider, but can I ask, please, if I, we, can count on your help to try and restore Plasmosid?" Power was hoping she would help. He had travelled thousands of miles now in the quest for some luck, some glimmer of hope against the darkness.

When she next looked him in the eye Power could see that

the news had broken her heart. "I have been guilty of the sin of pride," she confessed. "I've been busy jetting around the world like some Lady Bountiful, doling out small grants, and patronising Universities. Massaging my ego. And all I've been doing was providing some charitable front for a company that had rotted inside from its very core – and my two brothers have been plotting all this, for how long? Years, maybe. And they kept it all from me . . . let me jet around the world . . . on some ego trip . . . some self-aggrandisement. You can't know how it hurts. To see yourself as you really are."

Power decided to try some encouragement to spur her into some positive action. "Those grants, the beneficiaries like Universities. All that work was vital. Not just a front. Your work will bear fruit. And you still have control of the company don't you? You can right some of these wrongs. That is my hope. And to his great elation he listened to her next words.

"That is the only thing I can ethically do now. We come clean. We see justice done. We use all the company's resources to undo the evil that has been worked." She saw that Power was smiling and she smiled too. "Thank you for telling me all this Dr Power. I am grateful for your honesty. Even if it takes all the life I've got left and all the resources of my company Dr Power I promise you that I will do everything I can to put things right."

Her head exploded.

Blood splattered over the white wall in a spray of oxygenated bright red. Small gobbets of pink brain and white skull shot over the patio and plates on the table in front of Power.

Power let out a shout of alarm and horror and his legs almost involuntarily straightened in panic and he catapulted backwards, falling backwards in his chair just as a second bullet went whizzing in front of his face, missing him by just a few millimetres. His flailing feet hit the table, and it fell over too; plates, glasses and cutlery smashing to the ground. There were screams from people around. Marianne's limp body slumped to the ground with a thud.

From his vantage point on his back, on the floor, Power saw a male figure about six foot away, a grey hoodie covered his head, but the identity of the man Marianne had earlier seen playing with the dog was now clear. Cousins was frantically trying to unjam the Glock. The third bullet had failed to come out of the magazine and into the chamber. This gave Power a few seconds. Almost under his hand was the wickedly sharp pizza knife. Guided only by instinct and naked fear Power moved faster than he had ever done before. In two strides he was upon Cousins and with a terrific roar of rage he collided with the murderer and knocked him to the ground. The handgun went flying, and Power was stabbing, stabbing, stabbing at the man beneath him. The blows were savage, almost unco-ordinated, but fuelled by a towering rage that had burned in Power ever since he had fought Tuke for his own life on the cliff edge. The knife sliced into Cousins's deltoid muscle, cleaving muscle from bone. On a second blow, the knife pierced Cousin's ribcage, just below his clavicle, deflating his left lung in a pneumothorax. The third blow missed its trajectory as Cousins knocked Power's arm with a savage blow and the tip fell down, off the mark, into Cousins's face, and plunged into the orbit of Cousins's left eye, slicing the eyeball down to the optic nerve. A second person's blood spattered Power.

Then a young man, a passerby, who had run over and not seen the entire sequence of events, intervened. To him, from his limited perspective, it was Power who seemed wild, a knife-wielding maniac. The passerby caught hold of a half-empty bottle of wine from a table and slammed it against Power's skull. Power was floored. He slammed unconscious down onto the patio, his body half across Cousins.

The manageress, Aileen, screamed at the passerby to stop, that he had it wrong, that Power was innocent, a victim, but by then Power was unconscious and defenceless.

Sightless in one eye, in terrible pain, gasping for breath, Cousins was feeling around for the Glock to finish the job by killing Power. He too was caught up in a passion of anger, but a rational part of his brain was calculating. He could hear Aileen screaming that people should hold him, Cousins, down, as the murderer of Marianne Howarth-Weaver. To stop him getting the gun. And Cousins knew he was sorely wounded. He must use any remaining strength to run. He shouted at people to get back, that he had another gun, that he will kill anyone who tried to stop as he took flight, running from the restaurant, gasping with ragged breaths, in a desperate state towards the boat that waited for him.

TWELVE

Superintendent Lynch sat by the window in a comfortable armchair. The hours had passed infinitely slowly and as he watched the sunrise and the sunset he had ample time for reflection. Out of the window to his right he saw the bustling streets of Toronto. If he strained his neck, he could just glimpse the edge of the shoulders of the Toronto policewoman who sat just outside the private room at St. Michael's hospital. To his left Lynch could look at the bed and its pale, still occupant. Dr Power breathed slowly, steadily, but did not move. Occasionally a troubled frown furrowed his brow. He had been unconscious all the while that it had taken Lynch to rush to the airport, fly across the Atlantic and hurry by taxi to the hospital where they had taken Power. A small ring of empty Tim Horton coffee cups surrounded Lynch's feet. The nurses had suggested Lynch go back to his hotel and rest, but although more than twenty-four hours had passed since he arrived at the hospital Lynch would not end his vigil. His only absences from the room were the briefest of trips to the toilet.

An open Bible sat on his lap, and Lynch had been meditating on a single verse in Genesis:

> And for your lifeblood I will surely demand an accounting. I will demand an accounting from every animal. And from each human being, too, I will demand an accounting for the life of another human being.

Lynch had not been silent or inactive though. He had interviewed and been interviewed by a range of Toronto detectives and uniformed officers. He had personally seen all the statements from witnesses of the assassination of the Howarth-Weaver Chief Executive, Marianne Howarth-Weaver. While Power slumbered, dead to the world, his friend had been defending his character against unjust accusations and protesting, vehemently and surely, his friend's absolute innocence. And so assured had Lynch been, and so convincing was he of the danger that Power was in from a future attack, that the Toronto police had taken the unprecedented step of deputising Lynch and issuing him with his own firearm.

Lynch fell to thinking about what kind of accounting system would account for all the blood spilled by man. It would be vast. He prayed that God had a system that was perfect, and that would mete out and fit justice fairly and exactly according to the crime. He hoped so, for, in his experience, victims did not always see the perpetrators of crime receive true justice. The police issue revolver sat heavily in a holster on his chest. English police officers did not traditionally carry arms. The feeling was unusual for him. Would he use it if it were called for? If Cousins or another came here now to finish Power off, would Lynch use the gun to threaten, to ward off an attack or shoot the gun in anger, or dispassionately to defend. If he killed a man in the line of duty, could he live with himself as an officer, or as a Christian. The gun weighed heavily against his heart.

Power opened his eyes. The light in the room was

September grey, the windows long and reached down to the floor. A man sat by the bed; head bowed over an open Bible. He recognized Lynch.

"Am I in England then?" Power asked.

Lynch turned to him and smiled. "No Carl, still Toronto, for now. Home to England in a week or so, maybe?"

Power nodded silently and closed his eyes. And slept.

When he opened his eyes again, it was the night and the city was twinkling away outside his window. A sidelight was on, and the room was dimly lit. Lynch was looking at him over a tray of food. "Would you like something to eat, Carl? The doctor said it would be all right. I'll call them. They want to examine you." He offered the tray of food and Power struggled a way up and fell back against his pillows.

"The food is a nice idea, Andrew, but no . . . not yet. Thank you." He fell back against the pillows. His head felt as if it was full of wet sand, and it ached on the dry beach of the pillow.

The doctors came. Lights were shone in Power's eyes. A neurological examination including the sense of smell with peppermint and soap, and using reflex hammers on his tendons and pins on his fingers and toes was performed. The doctors seemed pleased, which in turn pleased Dr Power. He was asked what day he thought it was. He didn't know. He was asked where he thought he was. He thought it was a hospital in Toronto. He managed to recite the months of the year in reverse order, to do some basic maths, to recite the names of various flowers, the name of the Prime Minister. He winced as he said Blair's name and was asked if he was in pain.

Then Power was asked what he last remembered, before the hospital. Lynch leaned forward.

Power became visibly agitated. "Lunch on the Islands. A sunny day. With Marianne. I had explained everything. She took it reasonably well. She believed what I said. It must have been so very difficult for her. Then she was gone – like an insect smeared on a windscreen. He shot at me . . ." He looked at Lynch wide-eyed. "He only just missed. Because I fell backwards. I could feel the hot whistle of the bullet . . . on my nose. Going past."

"It's okay," said the doctor, and she patted his hand. "I don't want to upset you. I just wanted to know if you remember up to when you were hit."

Power looked up at her. "You're testing for brain damage. For organic amnesia." She nodded. "Well, I remember the impact. On the side of my head. I was . . . stabbing . . . I couldn't stop . . . the rage inside was . . . is still there. What did I get hit with?"

"A half bottle of wine, I was told," said the doctor. "Look, you need to rest. I don't want to take you through . . . events . . . just to know you have memory up to the impact is all I need to know for now. Tomorrow we will do an MRI scan, Dr Power. Make sure everything's in order, and then maybe you can be discharged. Until then you have your guardian angels to watch over you." She nodded towards Lynch and the Toronto police officer outside. "So rest well."

Power looked at Lynch, "You came all this way?"

"And why ever not?"

"How long have you been here?"

"A day or so."

"Have you slept? Have you got a hotel to go to?"

"I could only be at peace here. I have been occupied, don't worry, either reading or at prayer. "

"Is Cousins dead?"

"You didn't kill him straight away, that much we know, I mean he's still alive as far as we know. He flew from the scene." And Lynch was surprised that Cousins could have walked let alone run after Power's defensive attack. He had seen the CCTV footage on a laptop that the Toronto officers had shown him.

"Where is he then?"

"There has been an international warrant out for his arrest from when you phoned me from Peru. But a man like him probably has many identities. You were knocked out by a well-intentioned, but misguided passerby. Cousins managed to get up. He looked for the gun. Then he probably realised that there was no time for him to . . . and he ran. The gun has prints on, probably his, but the Toronto police can't match them to anybody on our shared databases. There was a trail of his blood. Group B, for what that's worth. It leads to the quayside. There's no record of any hospital in Toronto treating a man with . . . similar injuries that day. I suspect a boat had been waiting for him and took him away. Police have checked hospitals in towns and cities around the lake – Hamilton, Ajax, Burlington, even New York. But I suppose there are always private clinics who do work for people who don't want any questions asked. From what I saw Cousins won't be able to try again. Whether he would even survive . . . I don't know. If his partners, who picked him up in the boat, felt he was a liability . . . well, his body may well be somewhere in Lake Ontario. The aim was to stop you talking, so they could stay free. And here you are, able to talk as you like. And the more you talk, the less point there is in trying to stop you."

"Have the brothers been arrested?"

"I have tried to be as . . . Persuasive . . . as I can be, but the point of using middle-men like Cousins to do your dirty work is that the trail back to the brothers . . . is not easy to prove. And without proof . . . it would be a very brave and foolish US FBI officer who arrested two of the richest men in the world. They can be questioned about their sister of course; that would be a legitimate and routine practice. But that is not an arrest."

"But while they are free . . . they will want me dead. They would stop at nothing. They even killed their sister." Power said this numbly and distantly. His fingers gripped the sheets tightly and betrayed his fear. Power closed his eyes as if to blot out his anxieties. Lynch had never seen his friend as frightened before.

Lynch settled himself down in the chair to watch the door through the night. "Trust me now; you lay down in peace and sleep. I know you have difficulty in believing, but I have faith for us both. 'The eternal God is thy refuge, and underneath are the everlasting arms: and he shall thrust out the enemy from before thee; and shall say, Destroy them.'"

* * *

On the second day after Power had regained consciousness he was discharged. Power and Lynch took up rooms at Power's hotel. Power was edgy on his journey from the hospital to the hotel and refused to dine anywhere but his own room. On the third day after he had regained consciousness Power felt well enough to give the police the formal statement they needed.

Of Cousins, there was no sign, alive or dead. Marianne's body had been flown to New York for her brothers to mourn over in a lavish funeral at Sleepy Hollow Cemetery. After Marianne's assassination, the financial papers recorded the merest flicker of a downturn in the share price of Howarth-Weaver, before the share price continued the inexorable rise of recent weeks. The Howarth-Weaver corporation anointed brother Michael as CEO and its PR departments across the world announced the reassuring message that all was 'business as usual'. The financial pundits obediently believed the message they had been fed.

On the fourth day, after clearance from the Toronto investigating officers, Power and Lynch left Toronto. Power watched the ground falling away from them. Insulated and remote in his plane seat at thirty thousand feet he felt safe for the first time in days. He found he was able to concentrate and enjoy an in-flight version of Jurassic Park. Lynch chomped his way through the airline chicken. Power looked at both the chicken and vegetarian options with distaste and nibbled dry biscuits with tomato juice. He wondered why he only ever craved and drank tomato juice on planes.

They landed at Manchester seven hours later and Lynch and he took the airport bus to the car park, where Lynch had parked his Audi A6.

Power was looking forward to the short ride to his home in Alderley Edge when Lynch explained that he had no intention of driving Power to Alderley House.

"That's where they can find you, Carl. It's not safe yet. It will be safe again one day, but not today."

Power sank into the leather of the seat and looked into the distance. "But when will it be safe?"

"When the Howarth-Weaver brothers are arrested. When we have found the information they are trying to hide from us and when we have spread it so far and wide that they cannot possibly contain it. Until then, you must hide, and keep safe. And I know just where to hide you." He switched the engine on and began to drive them west on the M56 motorway.

The busy M56 looked small and narrow to Power after his time in America, but soon they were on even narrower A roads, through country towns like Oswestry and Whitchurch and into the county of Shropshire.

"They call it the Shire locally," said Lynch proudly. "Like it's some offshoot of Tolkien's world . . . you know, the *Lord of the Rings* . . . or *The Hobbit*."

"I don't know Shropshire very well, "said Power, looking glumly out of the window. He had been banking on getting home to Alderley House and slamming the solid wood door behind him.

"It's like going back in time," said Lynch. "To an England of twenty or thirty years ago."

"And where am I being spirited away to, exactly," asked Power, as they passed a sign to the medieval town of Shrewsbury. Lynch was driving down a narrow road, lined with timber-framed buildings - now housing cafés and gift shops. They crossed the River Severn over a stone bridge with four arches, and Lynch drove doggedly past Rowley's House and up the hill into the town centre, before dropping onto a southerly road that dwindled into country lanes.

"A village that time forgot," said Lynch.

Power shot him a look, "It sounds like the title of a film I wouldn't want to see. Where, exactly?"

"Heath. Some miles from here in the Clee Hills area, remote. A few houses. An ancient Norman Chapel. A farm maybe. The last time there was a village there was around the thirteen-fifties."

"What happened?"

"Something medical," said Lynch. "The great plague; the Black Death."

"Oh, a cheery place then," said Power. Lynch merely raised an eyebrow.

"The point is, Carl, that it's off the beaten track. Nobody will trace you here. And my sister lives in one of the houses. She wants to take you in and look after you."

"I don't think I've met your sister . . ."

"Valerie? No, well, it's not that we don't get on . . . but we don't always see eye to eye . . . on things like matters of faith, shall we say. We do get on generally, really."

Power sank deeper in his seat and wondered just how welcome he would really be. Lynch wanted to hide him away, but Power wanted to hide in quite another sense of the word – hide himself from everybody; by locking the doors and curling himself into a ball away from everybody, not feeling obliged to make polite conversation over endless cups of tea.

They left the A49 and Church Stretton and went east across the countryside along winding, country lanes that were so narrow that it seemed there was hardly enough room for Lynch's Audi to get between the hawthorn hedges and high muddy banks on either side. Periodically, Lynch had been checking his mirror to see if they were being followed, but this had not been necessary for many miles. There was no traffic on these roads. Power wondered if there had been no traffic since the year thirteen-fifty.

And then they had arrived. It was an early evening in September, and the sun was still in the sky, golden in a gorgeous pink sky streaked with red at the onset of night.

Lynch's sister's house was a two-storey, stone built farmhouse, built end on within the cleft of a fork in the track. To Power the farmhouse looked over two hundred years old. Lynch's A6 came to a halt outside a low wall that surrounded a small herb garden and the door to the kitchen. The half door opened to allow a stout middle-aged lady through, accompanied by two barking miniature dachshunds and a young teenage girl in tow. A boy, perhaps twelve or so, looked moodily out of the leaded kitchen window at his uncle. The entourage bustled through a gate in the wall and surrounded the car as Power emerged. He and Lynch were enveloped in a flurry of hugs and jumping, yapping dogs.

"Carl, this is Valerie. Valerie, this is Dr Carl Power."

"Please call me Carl," said Power.

"Come in, come in," said Valerie, and her voice had a typical warm Shropshire accent. "Don't stand about. Andrew, bring Carl's bag in. I understand you're fresh off the plane?" Power nodded, mollified as the entourage moved, like a Royal progress into the red tile-floored kitchen. There was the warmth of the Aga and a smell of good food. Power's bags were taken into the outhouse with an "I'm sure you won't have had time to do your laundry. I'm putting a load on now as it happens." Before he could protest, Power was seated in a tall-backed, but comfortable wooden chair by a fire and a glass of home-brewed ale was pushed into his hand, followed by a tray of vegetable and barley stew, with a hunk of buttered brown sourdough bread. In the chair opposite him, Lynch was treated similarly.

Power set to hungrily and then looked up. "How did you know I was vegetarian, Valerie?"

"Ah, well you'll only get vegetarian food here, see, as we're all vegetarian." Power smiled the broadest of smiles, and somehow the atmosphere of the country kitchen began to relax him in body and mind. The fire was bright and warm and now in marked contrast to the darkening sky outside. "Of course Andrew isn't vegetarian . . . we don't see eye to eye on all things. I won't have none of his religion either."

Lynch began to protest, "My 'religion' as you call it, is Christianity; and your family has . . ."

She shushed him in a way that Power had never seen anybody shush Superintendent Lynch before. "This is my house, Andrew. My rules. I've had enough of religion to last me several lifetimes, what with my grandfather and father and then you going on. You're all dinosaurs. Just eat up and enjoy your food and drink, Andrew."

After the stew was a gooseberry fool with the sweetest and mildest of lavender biscuits to accompany it. And then the tiredness washed over Power like a blanket muffling his strength and concentration. Valerie stood up and showed him to his room in the eaves. A comfortable old single bed with mounds of soft quilts stood on a polished wooden floor underneath heavy timbers that made up the cruck frame of the house. He couldn't remember saying anything like good night to Valerie. He didn't remember her helping him into flannel pyjamas like a child. He tumbled into the country bed, and before she even switched off the landing light he was fast asleep.

In the kitchen, when her children had left to go to their own rooms, Valerie fixed Lynch with a gaze. "Carl was exhausted. Just what has he been through? What have you done to him? What do I need to know?"

"I suppose, as ever, it's battle between good and evil," said Lynch, and at this Valerie rolled her eyes.

"Spare us!"

"Well, I think it is, a battle between healthy minds who try to alleviate human suffering and others who put profit first, for whom money is sufficient cause to betray any other human being and even their own family. If that's not evil . . . I don't know what is." He looked at his sister who was frowning at him. "Okay, Carl has been trying his best to follow up on a case. It was him that first saw that a case of suicide was nothing of the sort. That someone was trying to cover something up. That a company was trying to smother all trace of a new drug, in favour of a more profitable product. And worse they were prepared to cause thousands of people to develop an illness so they could sell that product instead of the drug." Lynch looked into the fire. A log snapped and cracked apart and a shower of sparks flew up high into the chimney. The scent of woodsmoke and the flickering light on the kitchen flags took him back to many years before. He struggled not to slip back into the past, and to stay in the present to answer Valerie's question. "Carl's been travelling the globe trying to piece it all together and to try, against the odds, to restore this lost drug. He's tried. He's battled. You see it is a battle. He's gambled everything; his job, even his life. And it's failed. So you see he needs and deserves a lot of help."

Valerie paused and poured out another coffee for her brother. "The news sometimes does filter through to the Shire," she said. "And I reckon that you're talking about malaria. The outbreaks across the world, and in Europe. Where there hadn't been none before."

"Well, I gather that malaria has been everywhere . . . even outbreaks in Russia a century or so ago. But yes, you are right. These outbreaks – a new strain – Carl and I suspect that they are . . . manufactured."

"Can you prove it?"

"We will, I hope."

"So you've brought me a broken man to heal, what else? What are you hiding him from?"

Lynch mused on whether his sister should have been a detective instead of him; whether she had missed her true calling. "Until we can defuse it all, prove our theories are correct, the culprits remain at large, and I don't want them to find Carl. He won't be found here."

"No, even you have trouble finding it. When were you last here? Two years ago?" She smiled. "I will look after him for you. He seems a nice enough lad. And if anybody comes looking for him I'll set the dogs on them." She looked at the two tiny dachshunds on her lap. They eyed her with their big, brown eyes. "Maybe we'll just have to hope that you haven't left any trail to us, Andrew."

"I'm sure that I haven't," said Lynch. "I didn't mention my plans to anyone except you. Even Carl wasn't in the know."

"He was asleep even before I closed the door; he must be exhausted."

" Hmm, as in Mark Chapter 6, Verse 31."

Valerie sighed, "Whatever made you so religious, Andrew?"

"Nature and nurture, I suppose."

"Well, I learned my Bible at our grandfather and our father's knee, like you. So I had the same nature and nurture Andrew, but I didn't grow up believing it. My opinion is that religion simply divides mankind."

"But that is a characteristic of mankind, not of God, it's our characteristic to form different tribes, and of course, the devil too delights in dividing us. God is bigger than all of us and bigger than all we imagine about Him. You seem to manage without Him. But I need Him to cope. I couldn't do what I do, see what I see every day, without Him."

"Well . . . maybe if some rather extreme people were a bit quieter about their religion . . . as it says in Proverbs – 'Whoever keeps his mouth and his tongue keeps himself out of trouble'. That's one I learned from our grandfather . . . "

"I try not to force my beliefs on anyone else, Valerie. And I'm very grateful to you for taking Carl in."

"You're both welcome, Andrew, any time. You know that. Would you like me to make up a bed for you too?"

Lynch was tempted to tumble into a bed and sleep the night away. He had slept little in recent days, but he was keen to get home to his wife. "I would love to stay. Spend some time. But I must get back. I will be back to get Carl, and maybe I can stay a bit longer when I return?"

He looked wistfully at the fire. It was dying down now; its glowing embers fizzing.

Valerie saw him out to his car. The light from the kitchen illuminated them both as Lynch kissed his sister and hugged her. "Thank you for looking after him."

"You drive carefully now. The lanes are twisty. Are you sure you're not too tired?"

"I'm fine," said Lynch. "I'll see you all again next time." And with that he climbed into his A6 and reversed out from the farmhouse into the lane, before heading off into the night.

* * *

The morning sun shone through the curtains in a tall, thin sliver of light onto the pillow where Power's head lay. He opened his eyes slowly and wondered where he was for a moment. Someone had kindly laid out a dressing gown on the chair next to his bed. He put this on, over his unfamiliar flannel pyjamas. He felt like a little boy again. He parted the curtains and looked out of the window over the fields. The trees were turned gold by the sun, but their leaves were also turning brown. It was Autumn in England.

Power put on some slippers that had been placed near the door and walked down the stairs. He smelt toast, eggs and coffee and smiled.

In the kitchen, Valerie's family sat round the table. Both children were in uniform and finishing their breakfasts. The two dachshunds barked ineffectually at him and retreated behind their mistress.

Valerie smiled at him, "Good Morning, Carl. Did you sleep well?" She placed a plate of eggs, mushrooms and toast on a placemat by him. "Sit down, I'll pour you some coffee."

"Thank you, I slept very soundly thank you. It was so quiet."

"That's true, nothing ever happens here," said Robert, Valerie's son. "It's a wilderness."

"At night, it's very quiet," said Valerie. She was placing home-baked fruit tarts and pies in a large wicker basket. "And of course there's no light pollution in the sky. No big cities around here."

"I live in Alderley Edge, usually," said Power. "It's quiet at night, but there's light pollution from Manchester."

"We've got an Edge too," said Sam, Valerie's daughter. "Wenlock Edge."

"It's a limestone escarpment," said Valerie. "About twenty miles long. You could walk there one day, maybe. There are walks around here too. There's a chapel. Heath Chapel."

"And that's it," said Robert. "That's all there is around here."

"And it's haunted," said Sam. Her mother glared at her.

Power thought that he would relish the quiet for a change. He began munching the buttered toast. "Thank you for this breakfast, Valerie. I'm not sure that I deserve this luxury."

"It's a pleasure," said Valerie. "And Andrew said that you are most deserving. Now, I'm sorry, but we must be bustling off. I have to drive the children to the main road so they can get their buses to school. Sam's off to the High School and Robert to Shrewsbury School. And then I am off to pick up some more produce from some of my cooks in the villages near here and then into town to open up the café. I'm taking these pies I baked last night. I hope you will be all right while we're gone. I've left a key on the table if you want to go for a walk. You could take the dogs with you if you like. Don't let them off the lead though. They will go down the rabbit and badger holes, and you'll have difficulty getting them out again. There are some books in the library, and there's a pan of soup on the side and a fresh loaf for lunch. Will you be all right?"

"Oh, absolutely," said Power. "No worries."

"Make yourself at home, Carl, and we'll see you this afternoon."

And with that Valerie was hustling the children out of the kitchen door and into a Volkswagen Golf that stood in a barn near the house.

Power finished his eggs and coffee. He stacked all the dishes in the dishwasher and switched it on. He was then struck by the thought that he didn't have any clothes. He wandered the house and found the snug, book-lined study. Valerie must have thought he would gravitate here because a range of freshly laundered clothes were airing on the radiator and his books, precious laptop and rucksack had been placed on the leather-topped desk. Making a selection of a t-shirt, jumper, boxers, socks and cargo trousers Power made his way upstairs to the bathroom. He relaxed in a hot bath for half an hour or so, shaved and dressed. Sitting on his bed in the attic bedroom Power once again tried to crack the password of the laptop and gave up after ten minutes. The sun was high in the morning sky, and he fancied a walk. He found a compass and an Ordnance Survey map of the area in the study and discovered the dogs' leads in the scullery. They trotted obediently over to him when they heard the rattle of the leads.

Power fixed the leads to their collars and after he had locked the house up they set off.

The sky was clear and cloudless. The autumn sun was weak though, and not much warmth could be derived from its bright rays. Together, Power and the two dogs sent off across the fields, over gates, and along hedges; all three of them sniffing the morning and drinking the air into their lungs. He heard a song thrush and caught glimpses of greenshank and plover. Power's map and compass reading skills were both exceedingly rusty, but on crossing various lanes between sets of gates he was soon picking up signs of the Chapel.

The ground now was uneven, at times raised up into earthwork platforms where houses had been or hollows where ancient fishponds had been. In the distance he saw, in splendid isolation, a small Norman chapel with roof intact.

He crossed a lane to a track that led over to the chapel. An angled English Heritage plaque stood nearby with pictures of how the Heath Chapel might have looked, when it was part of a busy Medieval village. He read:

> **Heath Chapel** – the perfect example of a rich little Norman chapel, built in the middle of the twelfth century, grey in siltstone rubble, with yellow sandstone ashlar dressings. The chapel consists of a two-bay nave with a south facing doorway and a two-bay chancel. The windows are small, and the doorway is decorated with chevrons. Wall paintings inside include St. George on the south wall, and the Last Judgment above the chancel arch.

Power made to carry on along the track to the chapel, a matter of two hundred yards or so, but the dogs would not have it. They barked; their hackles raised along their long and tiny backs, and they pulled backwards, resisting his pulling towards the building. There was no one about, and Power could not account for their evident fear. Eventually, the three of them reached a compromise and Power tied them up to post in the nearby fence, at which they were content, and he progressed alone towards the Chapel. They sat, as best as Dachshunds can, and watched him with anxious eyes as he strode over to the Chapel.

The door in the arched doorway was fast shut, although there was a sign which gave times of periodic services and suggested the Chapel was still consecrated. Another plaque stood in what would have been the graveyard surrounding the Chapel.

Power read it and suddenly began to feel the air around him as a chill wind. The sun was hidden behind the clouds. The graveyard of the chapel contained a small plague pit from the thirteenth century. Archaeological excavations found over two hundred bodies, of men, women and children within the pit. The plaque went on,

> Although there are records of a village prior to the thirteenth century, a visitation of the plague, or Black Death seems to have led to the abandonment of the settlement. This Grade 1 listed Norman Chapel is the only building to have survived, although nearby earthworks suggest that a busy, ancient and well-populated Medieval village surrounded the Chapel once upon a time.

Power looked about trying to imagine the cottages and farms in the landscape around him. The thoughts of infection suddenly striking the families and wiping out their village made him shudder.

The plaque further quoted the words of a Welsh poet Jeuan Gethin writing in thirteen forty-nine:

> We see death coming into our midst like black smoke, a plague which cuts off the young, a rootless phantom which has no mercy or fair countenance. Woe is me of the shilling in the arm-pit; it is seething, terrible, wherever it may come, a head that gives pain and causes a loud cry, a burden carried under the arms, a painful angry knob, a white lump. It is of the form of an apple, like the head of an onion, a small boil that spares no-one. Great is its seething, like a burning cinder, a grievous thing of an ashy colour. It is an ugly eruption that comes with unseemly haste. It is a grievous ornament that breaks out in a rash. The early ornaments of black death.

As Power stood there, the chill wind was picking up, whirling about him and tousling his hair. The air carried the sound of the dogs barking to him. They were calling his attention back to the present and for that he was grateful. He set off back to them. Power arrived back at the farmhouse in time for lunch. He sneaked a slice of bread and butter to the dogs and hoped that Valerie would not mind the indulgence. After lunch, he stacked away the dishes he had washed, read a while in the study, and then snoozed upstairs until he heard the busy sounds of the family returning after their day.

Power arrived in the kitchen to greet the family at the same time as the dogs. Everything was a flurried confusion of noise and Power realised how lonely he had been through the day. As they sat down to a cup of green tea and the children began their homework on the plain deal kitchen table and as the family discussed their day, a small bit of Power wondered what he would do with his time if and when he returned home. He had no job. Shouldn't he be making plans? He pushed the thought out of his mind and concentrated on listening to other people.

The daughter, Sam, was talking about a project about enzymes and the Kreb's cycle. Valerie's son, Robert, was mimicking his Scottish chemistry teacher. Valerie announced that the café, on Wyle Cop, had made record takings and that a very famous actor had enjoyed coffee and ginger cake in her shop.

Power asked if he could do anything to help make dinners. Valerie provided him with a pan of water, a chopping board, knife and a large bag of Shropshire potatoes and charged him with peeling and slicing spuds for a Pan Haggerty. He felt happy to be engaged in the family routine. Then they asked him what he had done with his day.

"I took the dogs out to the Chapel," he said. "They were generally very good, but they didn't like the Chapel. In fact, they refused point blank."

"It's haunted," said Robert. "I told you so. Didn't I tell him Mum?" The boy smiled at being vindicated. "Mum says she can see the people. The village folk."

"Oh Robert!" Valerie looked at her son disapprovingly. She looked at Power to see what he was thinking. "You can't say such things, especially when we have a psychiatrist with us!"

Power shook his head and laughed politely. "See them?" He asked, prompting her to say more.

"I just tease Robert that's all. Maybe I just have a strong imagination, Carl. Sometimes it feels as if the people are still there. In your mind's eye, of course. I don't actually see anybody clear-cut and solid."

"Well," said Power. "The dogs wouldn't go there, I know that. I don't have an explanation for why. I couldn't see or hear anything. Of course, dogs can hear more than we can. Maybe there was some infrasound or something. When I was growing up, I thought science could explain everything. But a lot of psychiatry is unexplained for now. Although it's getting clearer. Some psychiatrists thought schizophrenia was all in the mind, caused by mothers and their parenting. And now we can show there is an organic basis – actual changes on brain scans. So, the psychiatrists who propounded these theories were really quite damaging."

"And what do psychiatrists think of people who say they see ghosts?" asked Valerie, chopping up onions.

"There are a lot of possible explanations. Ghosts could be real. But that's a matter of faith. There isn't any real evidence, is there? Or they could be a product of a heightened state of emotion . . . like the bit in Disney's Snow White where the princess is scared and runs through the trees and in her fear the trees become monsters. They become alive. That would be an illusion. And then there's people with schizophrenia who hallucinate – hear things, see things that aren't there – but their hallucinations are as real as anything, and not triggered by fear or triggered by trees changing into things. And, of course, schizophrenia is an illness, which can be treated. But there are other descriptions of phenomena that are less easy. So there are times, when just after someone has died, when people see or hear that person. Like, after my uncle died, I was looking out of my study window and I saw him walking past. I was sure it was him. I put on my coat, and I rushed out, running down the road after him. But when I reached him I realized that it wasn't him. It was a man who looked a bit like him. Embarrassing. And then sometimes other people who have lost someone just hear a fragment of their voice in another room, or catch a glimpse of them out of the corner of their eye. And those events are called 'forced hallucinations of mourning', and are not abnormal. In other words, it's recognised that people can get these."

"I got those," said Sam. "After dad died." She looked at her mother, who had lowered her eyes. "After he had died I sometimes heard him coughing in another room, or smelt his aftershave on the air. It's normal then?"

"Very normal," said Dr Power. "And maybe it's our brain filling in the gaps, putting things in place that we want or expect to experience."

"Paul died two years ago," said Valerie. "An accident. Someone overtaking and going into his lane. Not his fault, and there was nothing he could do. I was angry with Paul, unreasonably. Angry with the other driver. Who just got a fine. Angry with Andrew, my brother, for not getting the other driver put away for life. Angry at Andrew's God." She sighed. But Andrew didn't give up on me. I suppose that's what families are for. Oh dear, I'm crying now. Is it the onion?" She went to wash her hands and busied herself at the sink, assembling the meal.

Power looked at Sam. She smiled feebly at him. Power tried to keep the conversation going. "Are you doing A levels?" She nodded. "What do you want to do at University?"

"Medicine," she said. "My grades are good enough. I just need to get some experience in a hospital, Accident and Emergency or something. Where did you train, Dr Power?"

"I trained as a psychiatrist around the North West," said Power. "But my University was Liverpool. I've spent some time researching and teaching at Manchester and Chester too."

Sam digested this information. "I have never thought about doing psychiatry. Is it difficult?"

"It can be," said Power. "People, like managers, don't understand it. The NHS doesn't invest in it. They just want to make savings. People with mental illness need practical support – sympathy and care – a roof over their heads – food – safety – and doctors too. But they're cutting our beds all the time."

"You wouldn't recommend it then?"

"I don't know. You'd expect that society would know better. The one organ that differentiates us from other animals – our brain – the one responsible for our thoughts and language and emotions and art and science – it's the area of medicine that society ignores the most."

"You don't believe in psychotherapy?"

"People need to be listened to, yes. But psychotherapy can't treat major mental illness. Major mental illnesses have been around for thousands of years. Talking therapies have been around for hundreds of years. There were ancient Greek physicians who thought people with delusions could be argued out of their illness. Listening therapy yes, we need that humanity in our work; but we need more than that. I didn't always think like that. I was very keen on psychoanalysis as a student. But if you spend some time with ill people, you realise they need services and treatment that is going to be there for the long haul. My view is not popular. People want to dismantle everything. I sometimes think I've been born into the wrong time."

And with that, Robert started asking Power to help with his mathematics homework, which Power did to the best of his ability. Dinner – Pan Haggerty and broccoli – followed. And after this and homework were complete the children insisted that Power and Valerie play a game of Risk with them. The four of them settled down in the lounge around a map of the world and for two hours battled, noisily, to take over entire continents. Power saw the evident enthusiasm of Robert later turning into a desperate determination to win the game. Power wondered, over a mug of coffee what it would be like to be a father himself, to have a son and daughter. Power battled on to ensure a fair fight and in the end, to his sister's grumbling concession, Robert won and went off to bed, cheering himself.

Before he climbed up into the attic bedroom, Power asked Valerie whether he could accompany her into town the next day. He offered to help in the café. He didn't want to be the guest that she had to wait on hand and foot. He wanted to contribute. He also did not want time on his hands, alone and waiting in the desolate farmhouse. He did not want to be left alone to think and to remember.

That night, Power was no longer exhausted. And so Power's sleep was not as deep. He woke at four in a sweat. A vivid nightmare about events on the Toronto Islands had put paid to sleep for the night. He sat up in bed and read a collection of poems by Dylan Thomas that was on the bedside table. He could hear them in his mind as if Richard Burton was reading them. Power loved the words in one of the poems – 'cobweb drum'. Given that he had just suffered a nightmare himself Power mused on what Thomas had meant by the phrase later in the poem:

My love as a round wave
To hide the wolves of sleep
And mask the grave.

The fears in his dreams – were they wolves? And did he usually mask his fear of the grave? Part of him drew grim comfort from the word and another part of him shuddered. He wrapped the duvet more closely about himself and watched the sun coming up through the bleak hours of dawn.

Power fortified himself with raisin porridge and coffee in the morning and set out in the car with Valerie and the children. His mood was brightening as the sun rose. The children were dropped off to await their buses and Valerie and he went to the farm suppliers to pick up a stock of bread, milk, flour, vegetables and potatoes for the café. They wended their way north through the villages of the Shire to Shrewsbury. The little and winding streets of the market town were already busy with traffic. Valerie parked up in a space behind the café, and they unloaded their provender into the kitchen. "We open at ten," said Valerie. "So we've got some time to set up." She sent Power round to check each table had enough cutlery, salt, pepper and napkins. Then she ran through the menu with him. She thought about showing him how to run the till, but Power looked confused enough.

"Have you ever worked in a restaurant before?" He shook his head and she kept her thoughts to herself. "Well, I'm sure you'll pick it up as we go. The customers are a friendly lot, by and large. If you can take their orders and wait on table, that will be a great help."

Everybody has their own talent. Power's talents did not include waiting on table. He was accurate in order taking and at times quite charming to customers, but in delivering the right food and drink to the right people he was too frequently haphazard. He was especially poor at handling more than two plates at once. His balance was poor, and at least two orders landed on the floor in a morass of sharp, broken crockery, cream and cake. After lunchtime both he and Valerie reflected on his first morning in the café and with relief on both sides, they decided his talents could be used better elsewhere. In the afternoon, he headed off to the Library and to numerous other coffee shops before it was time to go back to the farmhouse.

For the next week or so Power settled into a routine. In

the day he would take the dogs for walks, read, repair things around the house and garden, listen to music, prepare the evening meal, do homework with the children, laugh and discuss their day with the family, play games and sleep as best he could at night. Occasionally he phoned Lynch and asked for progress. One day he picked up courage to phone the medical director of an independent hospital and ask about whether there were any vacancies. He could not quite bear to re-visit the idea of working for the NHS. Not yet anyway. It had changed so much. The medical director was enthusiastic, polite, and advised him that the hospital was not a private hospital that catered to the worried well, but a fully equipped hospital that provided high quality care to NHS commissioned patients. He would certainly keep Power in mind for a vacancy coming up in December. Power put the phone down. He felt reassured that at least he had taken some step to rehabilitating himself. Occasionally he phoned Lynch hoping for news of progress and some hope he could return home. There was never any real news and Power began to wonder whether he would ever be able to go home in safety. Sometimes he thought he should take the risk and go home and at other times all he could see was the image of the Glock pistol firing at him, and the whistle of the bullet past his face.

One Sunday Power was reading in bed in the afternoon. The wind was howling outside and rain slashed against the windowpanes. Warm in his bed, and initially calm Power fell asleep.

Within an hour or so Power started dreaming. The grass

was a vivid, verdant green and it glowed unnaturally. The grass stretched seemingly forever under a marbled grey sky. In the middle, was the Heath Chapel. Round the Chapel lay hundreds of bodies – pale and pink except for loincloths. He wandered between the bodies. Men, women, children, grouped in families. Their bodies were still and lifeless. He inspected their faces and chests. The pinkness was a rash. He could see small lumps on their bodies. Though clearly dead, some of the bodies started shaking and shivering. He heard something, a bird, cawing. Then he realised that the sound 'caw' was actually his name being repeated, tauntingly: "Carl, Carl, Carl . . . "

He walked, or rather seemed to glide, to within a few yards of the chapel. Looking up, he saw a fat and oppressively black raven standing sturdily on the apex of the Chapel roof, dread monarch of all it surveyed. The Raven was calling his name. Power wanted to run, but some unseen force lifted him off his feet, up the wall of the Chapel and drew him closer to the Raven.

The right-hand side of the Raven's head loomed over him and with a sudden, shifting, sinking feeling Power saw that there was no eye in the Raven's head. The Raven's beak kept cawing his name. And then the Raven turned its head.

On the left-hand side of the Raven's head, a single eye fixed him with its glaring gaze. And the eye was a human eye with black pupil, iris and white cornea. Power felt constrained, strangulated as the bird spoke to him. The voice was redolent with hatred. "I know where you are."

And with that Power was awake, cold and slick with sweat, shaking.

He stumbled downstairs. It was late at night, but Valerie was still up. His distress was evident, and she hugged him tight. He was shaking in her arms as he told her of his dream. He felt like he was a child again. He explained his fears and his precipitate decision to leave. It felt like Cousins had worked his way inside his mind and had, for the briefest of time, looked into his soul. Power was overwhelmed with the irrational fear that his being with the family would draw Cousins to their home, and lead to disaster for him, Valerie and the children. He could not bear the anxiety that would now be associated with any decision to stay. He was for calling a taxi there and then to take him to a hotel in town. She was surprised by how violently the nightmare had taken hold of Power. She calmed him, made him a cup of tea, and rationalised with him late into the night. She stressed that there was no way Cousins could track Power. Only Lynch knew where he was. He would keep that information to himself. Power had no phone for anyone to trace. He had left this with Lynch. Power was safe, and Lynch wouldn't want him to leave. Power was adamant though. He couldn't bring anything on the family. He knew she was full of courage, but it wasn't fair. Eventually, she persuaded Power to stay till morning and promised he could then leave with her blessing, and not before.

He announced his need to leave to the children next morning. They listened tearfully and Power felt guilty. He offered to stay in touch, to offer them all dinner at his hotel while he was there and he invited the family to visit to Alderley when he eventually got home.

And so with a lift to town in the morning, Power left the haven of the farmhouse with Valerie's blessing, bade farewell to Sam and Robert at the bus stop. Valerie introduced him to the manager, a young man called Tim Jenkins, at the Lion Hotel in town and told him to give Power the best room he could. She seemed to know everybody. Tim was a tall young man with flaxen hair and a ruddy complexion. He was decked out in a full set of country tweeds and spoke with a friendly and calming burr. She also told Tim that it would be perfectly acceptable to register Power under a cover name in the register. She would vouch for him. He seemed perfectly happy to accept this from her. Power paid a week's rent in advance. Then, after she gave him a goodbye hug, she told him to ensure he would make good on his invitations to Alderley House.

Alone, in the high-ceilinged lounge of the Lion, Power slumped into a sofa with a welcome tray of tea and waited while his room was made up. At the reception desk, Tim finished registering Dr Power under a pseudonym as instructed by Valerie. He looked up occasionally at his new guest, nodded and smiled. Power clutched his bag of clothes and the laptop within.

Later, when Power was installed in his room, Tim received a transatlantic phone call from Superintendent Lynch who briefed him on how the hotel should deal with any callers , by phone or in person asking for Dr Power. For now, Dr Power was in residence at the Lion with the whimsical name, Mr Underhill.

THIRTEEN

There is thy gold, worse poison to men's souls,
Doing more murders in this loathsome world,
Than these poor compounds.

It was near dusk. While Jared was walking up 5th Avenue by Central Park in the gathering gloom he had felt, for the first time in days, that he was free of the watcher. As he turned onto East 63rd Street, however, he became conscious that he was being observed again, and his intuition proved to be correct, because there he was seated in the driver's seat of a Lincoln Navigator SUV on the opposite side of the road, his nose ostensibly buried in a copy of the *Wall Street Journal*. Jared stared at the middle-aged man, but the watcher did not flinch and did not look up. Jared made a mental note of the SUV's license plate, but this was an automatic reflex, and he didn't think he would do anything about the surveillance he was under. In days gone by he would have reacted – protested to the FBI, or asked Cousins to act on his behalf.

Seated in the SUV, Lynch watched his quarry via a CCTV screen rather than directly observing him. He hoped he looked less obvious this way, but he thought that Jared Howarth-Weaver was already well aware that he was being trailed. He watched the older man, walking down 63rd towards his brother Michael's home, carrying a small black box in his right hand.

For a moment, Jared paused at the doorway, then gained entrance and slipped out of Lynch's sight.

Inside the cream-coloured vestibule, he paused awhile for thought and gathered his courage. Then he was in the rich red carpeted hallway. Images of his tall, stout Canadian nanny swam before his eyes. He had always preferred her to his edgy, needy, imperious mother. Then one day, when he was due to go away to school, Nanny had been paid off, and she was seen no more. Leaving his life as finally and suddenly as if she had died.

Jared suppressed the other memories of his real family as best he could. Maybe, in retrospect, his sister had been the closest. Michael, whom he had spent most of his life with, had always been the bully. Marianne had saved his life once. Her good advice had always felt irritating. Now she was gone, and whom could he blame but himself, and Michael of course. He began to sweat, as usual, because of the sweltering heat of his brother's home.

"Where are you?" shouted his brother. "Skulking around down there like a burglar?"

Jared sighed and climbed the deeply carpeted stairs up to the first floor where his older brother stood on the landing. Michael slapped him on the shoulder and smiled. It felt false somehow. Michael pushed open the swing door on the landing and held it open so Jared could enter. As ever, the temperature went up a notch inside the doorway, and Jared accordingly shed layers of clothing and loosened his tie.

"We're in the study, as usual."

Jared followed his brother into the study and sat down on a high-backed wooden seat, opposite his brother. There seemed to be even more screens in the bank of financial information behind Michael's head. Michael waved at the flickering screens. "The Howarth-Weaver share price just goes up and up."

Michael switched on some extra lights from a console on the desk. "Getting dark early now."

Michael pointed to a whisky and soda with ice in it on the desk in front of Jared. "Drink up," he said. This was not usual. Jared always had to make his own drink. Michael sipped his own tonic water.

"How are things?" asked Michael, and smiled at his brother.

Jared carefully put the insulated black box he was carrying on the floor, under his chair, out of Michael's view. He unfastened a clasp on the side of the box and sat up. He looked at the whisky and soda for a moment and then swiftly drank it down with a determined look on his face. "Any more?"

"Help yourself," said Michael. He pointed to the drinks on the side and Jared went over. "You didn't answer my question about how things were?"

"What do you want to know?"

"Oh, I don't know," said Michael. "Perhaps you can reassure your older brother on how well you are getting over our sister's death. How are you coping with bereavement? It can be stressful. Heart attack rates go up after such losses. Or maybe I should ask a less emotionally charged question.

Maybe I could ask what artwork you have purchased recently? Or what you thought of that concert at Carnegie Hall that you went to."

Jared ignored these suggestions. "Cousins has disappeared."

"Does it matter?" asked Michael. I never really had to deal with him. That was your business. He sounded . . . odious. I suppose he's a loose end though. I don't like loose ends."

"That doctor, the one who was talking to Marianne. He's another loose end."

"Unfortunate, but he only has suspicions."

"I'm being followed," said Jared. "If you look out of the window you'll see a Lincoln. I've been tailed for days." Michael didn't make any attempt to go and look.

"Who by?"

"I don't know."

"Well, he's following you. Not me," said Michael. "Aren't you bothered? You don't look bothered."

"No. Actually I'm not bothered anymore. For the first time ever really."

"Oh well," said Michael. "That's good. Very good really. But rather strange for you. Did killing Marianne soothe you in some way? You're not troubled by a guilty conscience are you?"

"I can't do anything about that now. But I do think that I made the wrong decision."

"At least you admit that you killed her, that it was your decision."

"I see." Jared felt calm for the first time in many years. "I see you are shedding all responsibility."

Michael chose not to respond to this barb. Jared wondered whether Michael was recording the conversation. It didn't matter anymore, but Michael didn't know this yet.

"After we're gone," said Jared. "Who will get the company? Will it be Simon?" Jared pointed to the small black and white photo on Michael's desk.

Michael shuddered. "He's an idiot."

"He's your son . . . my nephew . . ."

"He's an idiot nevertheless. He came to see me recently. He's no better really. He hasn't matured a bit. He had many suggestions for you and me, for the company, all new directions. Worse than Marianne. He is an idiot. He probably gets it from his mother. It will be many years before he gets his hands on my company . . ."

"Your company?" Jared chuckled at his brother's hubris. "What direction do you think that you will take the company in?"

"Well, I've made it extremely profitable for a start."

"I guess I get the blame for Marianne, but not the credit for the rocketing share price then?"

"Oh, Jared. Don't be so bitter and twisted . . ." Michael scratched at his neck. An itch.

"Twisted?" Jared poured himself another whisky. His third. "A twisted loose end." He noticed Michael rubbing his wrist. Then scratching it. "Am I the kind of loose end that's also twisted?"

"You're not making any sense, Jared. You've had too much to drink. Go home." Jared laughed suddenly and unexpectedly which made Michael uncomfortable. "I'll put it down to grief, or whisky."

"I do regret what I've done. Do you regret the things that you've done?"

"As Edith Piaf said, 'Je ne regrette rien'. Which begs the question what do you regret, Jared."

"Well, I guess maybe you are taping this, Michael. But I'll tell you what I regret, for the record. I regret my sister was killed. I realise that I did an evil thing, and I miss her. If God exists I am sorry. I am sorry about what we did to suppress the drug. I hope you remember that we destroyed a drug that could treat treatment resistant malaria. We killed the good people who used their minds to try and heal others. I regret the suffering we caused. There can be no forgiveness, and there would never be any forgiveness for what we have done. I cannot fathom what led us to do what we did. I must have been a different person. Mad for a while. I find it difficult to believe we did it. But there is no doubt we committed the crime, and other people have paid, and will continue to pay. We let a bad genie out of the box. We did that. I did that. You did that."

Michael was blushing red. The barbs were too many and had sunk too deep to ignore anymore. "If I recall it was your division of the company that researched the malaria drug. Your division suppressed it. Your division researched the new strain of malaria, and also researched the more hardy mosquitoes. You were the link to Cousins. It was Cousins who killed the doctors. It was Cousins's team that spread the new mosquitoes and their resistant parasites. It was one of my divisions that researched the insecticide."

Fragments from a welter of childhood memories jostled in his memory. He mocked his older brother. "Come here, Mummy. Just look what Jared's done, Mum." Mother's dead Michael. No one cares what she would have thought. The world doesn't care what Mummy thought."

"But if the world should bother itself to look into our company. If they follow the loose ends. They will find that you're the one holding the other end of every loose end."

"And so I am myself a loose end that needs tying up . . ."

"I'm glad you said it," said Michael. "Well, as a matter of fact, yes you are."

"What was in the whisky then?"

Michael looked slightly discomfited. "Did you taste it? How did you know?"

"You've never made me a drink in my life. And I came here knowing I was a loose end you would want to dispose of."

"You just drank it down . . . and you knew . . ."

"What did I drink?"

"Ricin."

Jared nodded. He seemed to absorb the information intellectually. "Interesting choice. Not easily detectable. Unless I tell them."

"Hmm. Will you?"

"No. I won't say anything. Not for your sake, though."

"Then why? Why did you just drink it down? You knew it was poisoned. You drank it nevertheless. And now you tell me that you won't say anything. If you went to a hospital now and told them, you could probably be treated and survive. But you won't do that will you? Why?"

"Because we deserve to die."

"You mean you deserve to die."

Jared shook his head but would not be drawn further. Jared sat, just looking into his brother's eyes. Michael couldn't take the sudden honesty of that stare. There was no hatred, no malice in the stare. There was only finality – which terrified Michael. Michael realised that he had been seeking some sense of victory, but there was none. After all he had planned and done, something had gone wrong with the endgame. Like a game of chess that had seen the king taken, but because the rules had changed in a microsecond before the end, there was no victory.

Michael couldn't understand why. He scratched at his neck again. Damned itching. He looked down at his hand under the desk lamp. A flat, swollen white insect bite. And suddenly he understood.

Jared smiled at Michael as he saw the wave of comprehension wash over Michael's face.

Jared said, "It's only fair. If you think about it. We both go. Time for us both to go now. I'm resigned to it. You have a week or more to come to terms with it. And in a way you've done me a favour. Sped it up a bit for me. So, thank you for the drink." He reached under his chair and put the mosquito box on the desk. It was empty by now. Jared had a few bites himself, but the ricin would finish him first.

Michael said nothing. He was staring into space. There was nothing to be done, nothing to be said.

Jared stood up. Nodded to his brother and made his way out, down the stairs and into the vestibule. He put his coat back on. It might be cold outside.

As he closed the front door behind him and stepped onto the street he felt some pain in his chest, and he was suddenly breathless, like being smothered. The poison was taking effect more quickly than he imagined. Slowly he sank to his knees, clutching at his chest.

Across the road, sitting in the car, Lynch saw Jared slumping onto the concrete sidewalk. He got out and, dodging the traffic, hastened to Jared's side. The old man lay on his back, right hand clutching at his shirt. Lynch pulled a cell phone out of his jacket and dialed 911.

FOURTEEN

Power looked at the laptop. The black sign-in screen of the laptop looked back at Power. White letters on the screen flashed and the silently blinking question 'Password?>' burned into his retina. How many hours had he spent looking at this now?

On the steep, city road outside his hotel window the clatter of refuse bins being emptied heralded the sounds of early morning.

Power, bestubbled and sitting at the desk in his dressing gown reached over and switched the hotel kettle on. Watching the steam billow upwards, he mused on a combination of words or numbers that McAdams might have used to generate an eight-character UNIX password. He poured the viciously hot boiling water onto coffee granules and absentmindedly tried sipping the resultant black liquid and exclaimed to no-one; "Too bloody hot!"

The Tudor floor above his head creaked as the unknown occupant in the room above began to rise. Power wondered whether Prime Minister Disraeli had put up with the noises of close human habitation when he too had supposedly slept in the same room in the Lion Hotel in the eighteen hundreds. Power's mind wandered as human minds tend to when idling. He hummed.

The lion and the unicorn
Were fighting for the crown
The lion beat the unicorn
All around the town.
Some gave them white bread,
And some gave them brown;
Some gave them plum cake
and drummed them out of town.

"Of course," thought Power, "in the rhyme the Unicorn was Disraeli, and the lion was Gladstone. So how did Disraeli stomach staying in the Lion Hotel?"

However, the white question on the screen blinked uncaringly at Power.

"Maybe," thought Power, "McAdams just thought about the disease he was working on?" He put the word malaria into the screen before realising that it was a letter short of eight characters. Disgusted with himself he tried mosquito, but the screen calmly rejected his input. "I loathe puzzles," he thought. "I hate them. Anagrams, brain teasers, cryptic crosswords you can all go to hell!"

Later, in the dining room downstairs, Power read through *The Times* for Wednesday 16th October 1997.

The front page catalogued with sombre detail the rising death toll in Southern Spain. The death toll for Andalucia stood at 2,057 fatalities registered with a further 780,000 cases diagnosed according to emergency aid workers. A picture showed a mother and child lying side by side in a hospital bed. Grey-faced and hollow-eyed they stared out at Power. Hope was expressed that the cooling October weather would come to the aid of the overstretched health services. A tropical disease expert was quoted as saying 'By November the temperature will dip below seventeen degrees Celsius, and there should be some respite. We pray that this will give us a break until April next year before the temperatures get back to a level that will sustain the mosquitoes and the *Plasmodium* parasites that cause malaria.'

Lower down the front page there was news of a row in India about a speech by the Queen and a report of a fashion show by Stella McCartney.

The waitress deposited a hot plate of scrambled eggs and salmon under Power's nose and replaced his coffee with a fresh, silver pot. Prints of eighteenth century hunting scenes with madly elongated horses jumping country hedges sat on the wood panelled walls of the dining room. On the tables around him, other guests munched happily on eggs and bacon and outside passersby on Wyle Cop attested to the beginning of a market day in Shrewsbury town. How quaintly English it all seemed and so far removed from privation and distress. At Power's elbow stood a grandfather clock, which had ticked steadily and reassuringly since before Power's own grandfather's day. And yet time was short. The malaria was spreading. The mosquitoes would advance further north the next year and further still the next. There was no guarantee of safety, even as far north as England. It had been centuries since malaria had visited these shores, but the fact that it had cast a pall over Power's breakfast.

Deeper inside the paper he came across an odiously praise-filled obituary for Jared Howarth-Weaver. The list of his various achievements in the field of healthcare for the now-global family firm annoyed Power so much that the waitress paused in her duties to ask if there was anything wrong with his relatively untouched plate of eggs and salmon. Power grunted irritably at her and then thought to soften his response with an explanation, "I'm fine, it's just something I read." He read to the bottom of the obituary and noted the final sentence:

> He is survived by the last of his family Michael, who is gravely ill in hospital, reputedly with treatment-resistant malaria.

At this, Power spluttered, and a spray of coffee covered the table. Nearby diners glared frostily at him and wondered why Power was smiling so broadly all of a sudden. "Delicious irony," he thought.

And just as suddenly inspiration hit him. McAdams had been a team player. He had given his life to save his team. Why would the password not reflect his cherished team?

He went through the names of the three doctors; Dr Fergus John McAdam, Dr Corrine Amy Lloyd, and Dr Marcus Zuckerman. Their initials would be F.J.M., C.A.L. and M.Z. Eight letters. Enough for the password: FJMCALMZ.

He leapt up from the table, picking up the laptop that he now kept with him at all times and hurried through the calm of the dining room and up the stairs into the creaking Tudor architecture of the hotel to his room. The diners, middle-aged couples and faded businessmen, watched him go and shook their heads. They thought him young and eccentric, possibly some absent-minded professor that had escaped from a University.

Breathless and full of hope, Power ran into his room, disturbing a Polish maid who was working in his bathroom. She retreated demurely and silently, and Power flopped down at the desk and opened up the screen. As ever the silent question 'Password?>' blinked at him.

He typed in FJMCALMZ and hit return. Nothing happened. He swore, because he was bitterly disappointed. He had been so sure this time. He wondered if he had mistyped and tried again: FJMCALMZ. No joy and, in fact, he felt slightly weak as if his chair had suddenly fallen into the wooden floor by six inches.

He would never break this code. He considered how foolish he had been even thinking he could.

Then he thought of the scientific paper that McAdams and his colleagues could have written. He could even see it in his mind's eye, set in type, in some Medical Journal. A worthy title. A list of author's names. An abstract. And beneath this solid columns of close academic text. How would the author's names go?

McAdams, F.J., Lloyd, C.A., Zuckerman, M.

He wrote the three names down on an index card. That was how they would appear on a scientific paper.

He then typed: MFJLCAZM.

Miraculously the dead screen became alive.

Power gasped in relief as the screen burst into colour with the advent of the correct password.

The blank black screen was suddenly filled with a background close-up colour photograph of a mosquito, its needle proboscis slid into the hilly pink skin of a victim. Beady inhuman eyes stared out from the screen at Power.

For a moment he sat there, not believing his luck finally.

Then Power began to take long-awaited control over Dr McAdams's computer. There were only two files on the computer's desktop. As if McAdams had pared everything down to the most vital components.

Power cautiously copied both to a disc he had ready.

Then he clicked on the first file on the desktop. It was a graphics file. The mosquito portrait was replaced by another three-dimensional image of a molecule, slowly rotating in space. Underneath was a complex organic chemical formula. Elements of carbon, hydrogen, oxygen, nitrogen and fluoride seemed to be present. It meant little to Power, but he knew this was the exact structure and formula for the drug McAdams was working on. It would be all that was needed to convey to a biochemist what McAdams's malaria drug was. The 3D model and formula to a biochemist would be just like the sheet music of a symphony penned by a genius would appear a competent orchestral conductor.

He minimized the image and clicked on the second file. It was opened by a word processing program.

The document was entitled:

The Clinical Efficacy of a Novel Drug Against Treatment-Resistant Malaria
McAdam, F., J., Lloyd, C., A., & Zuckerman, M.

Power read through the sections of the paper about the compound that McAdams called Plasmosid: Abstract, Introduction, Chemical Structure and Manufacture, Theoretical Pharmacology, Materials and Methods, Results of Clinical Trial, Efficacy and Recovery Data, Safety Data and Adverse Effects, Discussion and Conclusions.

It was all there. How to manufacture Plasmosid. The small open-label clinical trial they had done on thirty patients dying from treatment-resistant malaria in Asia. The recovery, against all expectations of more than twenty-five of them. In the discussion section, McAdams mused on how further trials were needed, but that if Plasmosid was employed earlier in the infection Plasmosid might save an even higher percentage of these previous doomed patients.

Tears sprang to Power's eyes. McAdams had died to protect this information and his team. But his team had been killed despite his sacrifice. And the information itself had come so close to being wiped out and obliterated forever. What must Power do now? Transmit the information. Disseminate it for everybody to use. And as quickly as possible.

He looked at the list of programs on the laptop computer. No Internet package. And no Dial-up or Ethernet sockets in the room. Power swore. He'd been using the Internet for a few years. Why couldn't other people see the point yet?

He phoned down to the Lion's reception. "Please. Is the manager there? Is there any Internet in the hotel? There's nothing in my room."

Tim Jenkins, the manager was on the desk, "No, Dr Power, I'm sorry. We're planning to have some sockets put in some rooms next year."

"Oh dear, it's urgent you see, can I ask . . ."

The manager interrupted, "Is it a medical matter, doctor?"

"Yes, yes," said Power. "It is. Life and death. Many lives actually."

"Well then,"said the manager, Tim Jenkins, rather taken aback by the alleged importance of the need. "I have my own personal Internet dial-up in my flat here. Can I help?"

"Yes, yes you can."

And Power was down the stairs at the reception desk almost before the manager had even put down the phone. In his hand, he clutched the disk with the files on.

The manager was quietly impressed, "Is it that important, really, Dr Power?"

Power nodded. He was shown through the archway at the back of the reception and into a pair of small rooms that the owner/manager used. "Sometimes it's difficult to get away," the manager explained. "Last night I was here till two with a private dinner. You can't face the drive back home at that hour." He showed Power to a brand new Viglen computer. "A 200 MB hard drive and Windows NT", he said proudly,

switching it on. He started the dial-up process, and the modem chirruped and fizzed into life. And Power was on-line, cranking up Internet Explorer and his webmail package. He logged in and paused. Who was he sending this to? He remembered his friend from University. The one who had emailed him with a list of graduates from his Year who had email addresses. He recalled how he had nearly deleted his friend's email. Now he feverishly copied and pasted the entire list into the 'To:' box of a new email message window. They would all get the email. He attached McAdams's two files to send alongside his words and wrote.

> Dear All, It's Carl. I hope you remember me from University? You haven't heard from me till now, and I apologise, but I must ask you for a really big favour. The attached files contain information about a new compound – a novel drug for malaria – and it's important it get to as many people as possible. That it's shared and not hidden away. Read the files and see if you don't believe me how important this is. And if you agree with me that this is vital, in the light of the news, please can I ask you to send it on to as many people as you can?
>
> If you send it on to at least ten people you know in medicine or health, then the information can find someone who can understand and listen and act and make this drug available. Please trust me and send this message on.

He pressed send. And he prayed for the first time, in a long time, that the message would reach somebody. That the message would spread and multiply, just like the parasite itself.

And then he went on emailing to anyone he could think of; the editor of the *BMJ* and *The Lancet*, his professor of infectious diseases from university days, the health editors of the BBC and *The Times* and *The Guardian.* He didn't notice the manager putting a drink of coffee and a sandwich at his side until he had finished. As he logged off, the coffee was cold.

"Thank you for letting me use your machine," he said, taking the disk from out of the manager's PC. The manager, Tim nodded, smiled understandingly and went to get Power a new pot of hot coffee.

Power's phone started ringing. The first of the calls about the paper. The phone didn't stop ringing for days.

Power and Lynch will return in Schrödinger's God

Music for Dr Power

A set of music has been suggested by readers; these suggestions accompany some of the music that inspired the author, Hugh Greene, whilst writing the original novels.
If you would like to suggest additions to this list please email the author via www.hughgreene.com

For The Darkening Sky

Darkening Sky (Peter Bradley Adams)

Leylines (Aes Dana)

Alignments (Aes Dana)

Sky Quest (Toby Langton Gilks)

Sky Strikeforce (David Hughes, John Murphy)

Sky Dark Orchestral (David Hughes, John Murphy)

For The Fire of Love

The Fire of Love (The Gun Club)

4 Sea Interludes by Benjamin Britten

For The Good Shepherd

The Dreamscape by Chad Seiter

Symphony No. 6 by Vaughan Williams

Mosquito by Yeah Yeah Yeahs

Mosquito by Flexness

Infra 2 Max Richter

Recomposed: Vivaldi Four Seasons by Max Richter – Spring 0, Spring 1, Shadow 2, Winter 2, Winter 3.

The Lord is My Shepherd (John Rutter)

Shepherd of Fire (Avenged Sevenfold)

Shepherd's Chorus (Contenti N'andremo) (Respighi)

Good Shepherd (Wovenhand)

The Chester Walls Walk

A key part of the Power and Lynch series is its sense of place. The mysteries are set around the county of Cheshire and counties nearby.

Fans of the series have popularised a walk around the Walls in Chester City centre that is featured in a key passage in The Good Shepherd. Chester was a Roman city based on a large military camp (Deva).

To do the walk yourself you will need to find the Roman walls in Chester. Perhaps start by The Architect pub (54 Nicholas Street, Chester, Cheshire CH1 2NX). The old police headquarters where Lynch worked in The Good Shepherd no longer exist, but the pub makes a more convivial starting (or end) point. Details of the walk that Power and Lynch take in the novel are below and also can be read in an extract from the novel. Other sites with more details of the wall exist.

> At the rear of the pub is Nuns Road. (There was a convent/hospital on this site in antiquity.) Walk along the road, away from the racecourse and Roodee and cross the A483.
>
> Begin walking the Roman walls, past the stumpy remains of Chester Castle on your left and the nearby Law Courts.

On the left is the castle and the University of Chester; on the right hand side the river Dee flows down below the walls.

Follow the walls to Bridgegate on the South Wall.

Stop on the Wall between Barnaby's Tower and Newgate and look out over the remains of a Roman courtyard and gardens.

Begin walking again towards Newgate and on to Thimbleby's Tower.

Cross the Eastgate of the Wall and on to the Kaleyard Gate. (Eastgate is featured on the front cover of The Darkening Sky.)

At Northgate a flight of steps leads down to the road that leads to the Cathedral where Lynch often worships. Go down the steps and into Northgate Street and find a cafe that Power and Lynch might like.

Alternatively carry on along the wall and it will take you on to the Racecourse and back to the 'Architect' for some refreshment.

Printed in Great Britain
by Amazon

31237037R00134